A Stop the Pre

Stop the Presses:

My Boss is My Fake Boyfriend

By Jade Anthony

You're not supposed to make up boyfriends, and you're not supposed to date your boss – but in baseball and in life, Contessa Toews has never played by the rules.

Stop the Presses:

My Boss is My Fake Boyfriend

By Jade Anthony

Special thanks to my family, my Mom, David and Trina for your encouragement and support.

.

Chapter 1 — Tessa

"Toews!"

I hear my last name bellowed – pronounced, incorrectly, as Toes – from somewhere within the depths of the office that to me, right this moment, seems more like a dark cave housing some sort of mythical beast. The Minotaur, or Jabberwocky, perhaps?

"Contesla?" says the quirky-looking Asian girl at the desk. She looks like an Anime character come-to-life, with the porcelain skin and exaggerated eye makeup of a Japanese Geisha, combined with the knee-length frilly-hemmed skirt, calf-high black leather boots and jet-black hair of a rockabilly pin-up calendar girl. She has drawn-on eyebrows, razor-sharp bangs and several visible tattoos of butterflies.

"Mr. Osborne will see you now."

I've never been crazy about my full name. In fact, at one point, in my teens, I had downright hated it. The other kids, especially the girls, mocked me with royal waves and fake curtsies. I imagined their faces on the baseball when I hit it. It could have been worse. Dad had wanted to name me Contesla, in honor of Nikola Tesla, inventor of the electric motor. Dad fancied himself a bit of a creative genius as far as inventions went. Right up there with Wile E. Coyote. More on that later.

To kids my own age, though, it would just have meant I was named after a car. Shelby or even Mercedes, Sadie, I could live with, but Contesla … not so much. It was times like this I was eternally grateful my dad hadn't driven a Gremlin. Or, worse, a Hummer.

My last name was just as confusing. It was of German ancestry and no one, repeat no one, knew how to pronounce it properly. Correction, almost no one. The Canadians up at Carleton University in Ottawa had known it was pronounced Taves, mainly, they told me, because they were such big hockey fans and a Canadian, Jonathan Toews, had captained the Chicago Blackhawks hockey team to a couple of Stanley Cup championships. Those canucks love their hockey.

I stood, making sure to grab both my purse and laptop bag. I barely remember to shut my cell phone off. I hate being this nervous.

Sandford Osborne, the great and powerful Oz himself, was seated behind a huge wooden desk. He didn't look up. He had snow-white hair cut in a 'high and tight' crew-cut and a bright red face. He reminded me of a Marine Corps drill sergeant with blood pressure issues. But then, on TV and in the movies, ALL military officers seemed to have blood pressure issues.

I wonder which came first: the crankiness or the high blood pressure. Kind of like the chicken and egg thing.

It was just an office, with regular fluorescent lighting, but to me it felt like being under the spotlight in a police interrogation room. I wondered where they kept the thumbscrews and water boards. I felt the tickle of a single droplet of sweat escape my armpit and make a run for it down my side. It was a good thing I'd put on extra deodorant this morning, I think, as I wait for them to bring in the lie detector machine.

I've always had a very vivid imagination. Thanks, Dad.

"Sit," he says, ignoring my outstretched hand. If he even noticed it he gave no indication. "So, Toews …"

"Actually, it's pronounced Tav-es," I say, pronouncing my own name wrong, hesitating on the last syllable, making it sound Hispanic, as I realize all too late that I had just cut my potential future boss off mid-sentence. Did it really matter what he called me? I just want the job. He can call me whatever he wants. Deep breaths, deep breaths.

Two ears, one mouth for a reason, Tessa, I told myself. Shut up and listen. And stop thinking so much!

"So, Toews," he repeats, pronouncing it incorrectly again, maybe on purpose. I wasn't sure what to make of him calling me by my last name, but it was … different

It was more like being on the ball field than in an office, which was perfectly fine with me. I had excelled at softball in high school, making the all-state team and, truth be known, would love to write about sports. I'd been good, but not good enough to warrant a scholarship to a U.S. college, hence the journey to Ottawa to stay with my mom's sister and attend Carleton. Factoring in the value of the U.S. dollar compared to Canadian currency, it was actually affordable without my parents having to take out a second mortgage.

"High school paper, yearbook club, co-captain of the softball team," he reads aloud off my resume. "I don't give a rat's behind what happened in high school," he growls, finally looking up. "Ancient history."

Okay, what am I supposed to say to that? A smile seems appropriate. It usually was. I wasn't gorgeous, but I wasn't ugly either. When in doubt, smile and nod, my dear old dad always told me. Just don't ever sign anything without reading it.

But then, he also used to tell me I could get into baseball games or get out of traffic tickets just by telling them "I'm Eddie Toews' daughter." I did try it once, to try to get out of a speeding ticket. I smiled. I nodded. I called the officer 'sir' and told him who my dad was. "Who?" was the response? And, one $100 ticket later, I never tried that again.

When I told my dad, he suggested another little trick that had worked for him in Palm Springs one time. He simply pretended he was from Canada and didn't speak English. Je ne Parle pas English.

He finally admitted that he spoke English, but claimed he forgot the speedometer was in miles per hour, not kilometers, when he was clocked doing 100 on the I-10. THAT one the highway patrolman believed. Only in California, dude.

So, I'm a little torn on taking my dad's advice these days. Osborne hasn't asked me a question, so I just sit there. Smiling. Better suck it up, buttercup, my inside voice tells me. Journalism's not for wimps.

"Journalism degree from Carleton, eh?" he barks, breaking the uncomfortable – at least for me – silence and looking at me expectantly.

"Yes, sir," I somehow stammer, unable to shake the drill sergeant image and feeling another drop of sweat meander its way down my side.

"It's a Canada joke, Tessa, Get it? Eh?"

"Oh sure," I say, forcing a smile that I was sure looked more like a monkey grimacing in pain than anything resembling human laughter. He'd caught me off guard with that one. Drill sergeants never joked in the movies. Who was this guy? Some kind of Jerky and Hyde?

Well, if the boss wants me to laugh at his jokes. I'd laugh. After all I'd been laughing at my dad's lame jokes for years. One of his favorites was: "I can tell a train's been here. I can see its tracks." A little bit funny the first time, no so much on the one-hundredth.

I look down and notice my feet are shaking, no vibrating. Like a jackhammer.

It was as if I'd taken some of the earthquake pills the good old Wile E. Coyote was always accidently eating in a valiant but ill-fated attempt to catch the roadrunner on one of my dad's favorite old cartoons.

My dad always cheered for the coyote. "Today's the day he catches the roadrunner," he'd say, every Saturday morning. He admired his effort and ingenuity. Coyotes were really smart, he says, and roadrunners are good eating. "Like a skinny chicken," he says.

I remember thinking, even as a small child, "If he's so smart, how come he thinks a toy umbrella will protect him from a falling anvil?"

I also remember being very hesitant about eating the Cornish game hen my dad brought home.

I was sure Osborne could feel my feet tapping on the floor, as they performed their own under-the-desk version of River dance. Probably the whole office could. If this were California, they'd be sounding the earthquake alarm and hiding under their desks. Which is what I wish I could do right now.

"Why should I hire you?" he asks, no, demands, out of the blue, point blank.

And there it was. No beating around the proverbial bush here. No fancy human resources questions like: "Tell me about a time when you saved the universe by blowing up the Death Star."

Screw that, I thought, I was dealing with saving my own universe, at least for the time being. Okay, Tessa, time to sell yourself – not exactly my forte, but here goes …

"Well," I begin, in what I hope is a confident and professional tone, "I'm a people person. I like working with people..."

"Great!" he says loudly, dropping my resume to his desk. "Because I've already hired someone to interview animals. That position's filled. Fella says he can talk to the animals. Doolittle's the name."

Okay, I thought, sarcasm. Was that really necessary? At an interview for an internship? I'd heard about this in journalism school. It was the way news people were. Just like cops had their warped sense of 'gallows humor', journalists were known for wielding words like weapons. Language was their gun and words were their bullets.

I knew, though many still liked to make the claim 'the pen is mightier than the sword', few truly wanted to put it to a literal test. A little verbal jousting was just their idea of having fun. It wasn't personal, but it sure felt like it. I could sling words with the best of them, including some that would make a sailor blush, but thought better of it.

"I want to make a difference," I say, forging ahead. "I think journalism is one way I can do that."

OMG! I sound like I'm in a beauty pageant not a job interview. No need to tell him yet I want to write about sports. No need for him to think I'm a complete ditz.

Everybody thought only bottle-blonde bubble heads wanted to cover sports. At least I wasn't blonde. Yet. But I could be if he wanted me to be.

I flashback to an early baseball coach, he'd told me I was too short to play shortstop. Talk about ironic. I looked him right in the eye and told him "I can play taller." And made the team.

Osborne's looking me in the eye now, his dark orbs boring into the depths of my very soul. Does this guy ever blink? What's he thinking? Do I ever stop thinking? Arrrgh! I sure wish I hadn't had that second cup of coffee this morning. I have to pee.

"Hmm," he grunts, obviously unimpressed. "Let me tell you something, Toews," he says, continuing to pronounce it as Toes. "It's all about the writing. And interviewing. Some people have it, some don't. I could take art classes the rest of my life and still not be able to paint a fence. You've either got it, or you don't. Do you have IT, Toews?"

"Yes, I ..."

"Have your best example of one written article and one video news report on my desk by 9 a.m. tomorrow morning. You can email them to my secretary, Suzi."

Secretary? This guy really was a dinosaur. Jerkosaurus Rex.

"Yes, sir," I say, wondering if I should salute and what portfolio pieces I might have that would ring this old coot's bells and whistles. If he still had any.

"I've also got a blog site and a Tik Tok following," I spout, hoping to impress him with my social media presence, "if you'd like to go online and check them out."

"I don't. I don't blog. I don't Tik and I don't Tok. That's why I hire you young people."

He picks up another resume. "Schmidt!"

I was dismissed, apparently.

I stop at Suzi's desk to get her email address.

"I think he likes you," she whispers, giving me a wink and handing me a card with her contact information. Suzi Kwan, Executive Assistant to the Publisher. Email: suziq@s-b.com.

"Thanks," I say, thinking, how can you tell?

And just like that, what seemed like the longest half hour of my life was over. No handshake. No "goodbye" or "have a nice day". No "thanks for playing". No lovely parting gifts. Nothing. I look at my watch. All of 15 minutes has passed. I guess it's true, time does fly when you're having fun.

Hmm, maybe I'll get the hang of this sarcasm thing after all.

Chapter 2 — Steve

Great, I think, glancing up, another spoiled brat intern to babysit. Just what I need.

The girl coming out of Mr. Osborne's office looks like all the rest. Young. Very young. Perky. Too Perky. They always arrived full of truth, justice and journalistic integrity, ready to change the world. But the idealistic deer-in-the-headlights phase wouldn't last long, I knew, and they'd soon be as jaded as I am. No not jaded, just … realistic.

A career in journalism could do that do you?

Especially if you work the crime or city news beats. They were called beats for a reason, because they could certainly beat you up if you let them. Talking to accident victims, interviewing criminals, lawyers and politicians – I like to group the latter three together – wasn't for everyone. Some grew immune to the constant tragedy, of continually encountering mankind at its worst, of being lied to, of being immersed in a cesspool of humanity. Some drank. And some simply couldn't take it and left.

Looking at this new recruit, I couldn't help but wonder which she would turn out to be – If she had a future in news at all. In any case, I was going to put her through the paces, that's for sure. In fact, I enjoy making life difficult for the interns. Might as well weed out the ones who can't handle the pressure right away is my personnel policy, and not waste any more of my valuable time than necessary.

That's what Mr. Osborne had done for me and now, two short years later, at the ripe old age of 20, going on 21, I was in charge of the City News department. I was younger than all of my direct reports and most of the interns when I was promoted, and still am – and I owe it all to Mr. Osborne. He gave me a chance and supported me when no one else would, and for that I will be eternally grateful.

Well, Mr. Osborne and my mom, Mary Sondergaard. She's always supported me. That's what mom's do.

I knew that the other employees called Mr. Osborne 'the Wiz' and the 'great and powerful Oz'. Behind his back, of course. And I also knew that they called me 'mini Oz', which was fine by me, and other, less flattering, nicknames. I didn't care though, because, well, I just didn't care. Never did.

I learned not to worry about that at a young age. I didn't fit in, the kid who didn't play sports. Who didn't play, period? "Sticks and stones may break your bones," my mom used to say to me as a child, "but names will never hurt you."

They could, I discovered later, just look at the effect social media shaming and bullying was having on young people these days – but as a child it was advice that served me well. Besides, Sandford J. Osborne is my hero. I want to be just like him, the sooner the better. No matter what it takes, no matter what people say.

I'm well aware that Mr. Osborne is the father figure I never had. A substitute. I'm also aware that he cares about people more than he lets on. No one else knows. Just me, Mr. Osborne, and his wife, Jenny. And I'm sworn to secrecy.

I was just over a year old when my mom was diagnosed with Multiple Sclerosis and my dad left. Forever. I have zero recollection of him and my mom made a point of never showing me any photos. He didn't even stick around long enough to see if she was the relapsing/remitting kind, or progressive.

With relapsing/remitting MS, the person may experience a certain degree of loss of function in terms of walking and other physical mobility, usually accompanied by 'pins and needles' or a tingling sensation in the extremities and frequent fatigue. Given the proper treatments and lifestyle, these people can be quite functional in terms of driving, working, raising a family, etc.

Progressive MS, on the other hand, meant just that – it was a steady slide downhill until the person was eventually wheelchair-bound, institutionalized and died from various related causes, often related to breathing difficulties.

As it turns out, my mom has both kinds. For the first few years, she was okay. She was able to work just enough to keep a roof over our heads and food on the table. Every day she came home exhausted, ate a quick dinner and then slept from 7 p.m. to 6 a.m., when she'd get up and head off to work again.

I got myself breakfast. I got myself dressed and off to school. I did what housework I could and tried to do the yard too. We had good neighbors and they let me use their smaller electric lawn mower when they saw me struggling to start and then push our big old gas guzzler. I started doing several of the neighbors' lawns for $20 each week and bought the mower from them. I was eight.

I guess some people would label me as OCD, or a workaholic, but I just saw it – and still do – as doing what needs to be done. What else was I going to do? Sit around and watch cartoons? There's nothing wrong with having a strong work ethic, I thought. And I still do.

So, I'd assumed the role of man of the house – self-appointed – when I was five or six and accepted the responsibility that comes with it. I cooked the meals – my specialties were grilled cheese sandwich, macaroni and cheese and chicken noodle soup – I paid the household bills, picked up the mail and either made or arranged for any other maintenance to be done. Google was my best friend. This added accountability, I was later told by a child counselor, is likely what triggered my moderate compulsions into more intense obsessiveness. For example, only Heinz ketchup went on the grilled cheese, only Kraft Dinner mac and cheese (and only the original mix) and only Campbell's canned soup. Nothing else would do. I would literally go hungry before I used a different brand. Nothing else would do. I ate nothing in sauce or anything mixed together. Ever. I was also a 'gifted' child, I was told by the same counselor. Funny, I didn't feel gifted. If anything, I'd been shafted, cheated out of any semblance of a normal childhood. Of course, I didn't know, or care, at the time. I was very happy in my busy little world with my good friend Mr. Google. Mr. Google knew everything. Who needed a dad when I had Mr. Google to teach me everything?

Since then, it had been a whirlwind of skipped grades and early graduations. I finished elementary school at nine, high school at 15 and university at 18. Needless to say, the other students weren't interested in hanging out with a baby-faced teen – heck, I was going on 21 now and still only shaved once a week.

Growing up with Mr. Google had piqued my natural curiosity, so I signed up for a degree program that would let me learn about a wide variety of topics, not specialize in any one area. One that would encourage me to ask lots of questions, because I needed to know … everything.

The Minnesota Journalism Center had been established in 1979 as part of the University of Minnesota's Rochester campus and it soon became my second home.

I may not have had friends, and I never played any sports, but, in between household chores, I did find time for a hobby, one I enjoy to this day – earning money.

I started delivering flyers for the local paper as soon as I learned to ride a bike at five. Soon, I found myself managing several routes, paying my elementary school classmates a percentage to do the actual delivery while I managed collections.

Mom made enough money to pay our bills back then, but even as a kid I knew things were tight. We didn't take vacations. My mom never went out to dinner or shows. She never used the Internet, and it cost over $50 per month for service, so I thought I should at least contribute to that. And didn't I eat the groceries too? I usually went and did the shopping with money she'd leave me on the kitchen counter, $100 a week, but here was no reason I shouldn't contribute to the cause.

When I met Sandford Osborne, I was in awe. This was who I, Steve Sondergaard, wanted to be. Mr. Osborne didn't care if people liked him. He didn't need you to be his friend. He didn't have time to waste on silly human emotions or drama. He. Just. Did. His. Job.

I knew my mom didn't really agree. She thought I needed to relax a little, make some friends, get a hobby, and maybe even find a nice girl. She wasn't, still isn't, crazy about me turning out like him. I think she'd prefer I model myself after somebody nicer, like Ellen, or Oprah.

"They're women, Mom."

"I know, but they seem so nice."

What do you say to that? To your mother?

"Do you like girls?" she had once asked me, as the Beatles' She Loves You played in the background. The Beatles had been the soundtrack to our lives. It was all she listened to and by five years old I knew the words to most of their songs by heart. Too many were about love, in my opinion.

"Sure," I had replied, more to appease her than from any sense of reality. In truth, I thought they paid too much attention to outward appearances and talked too much. Seemed to me like they wasted a lot of time talking. A lot. Like my mom was making me do right now. Talk about feelings. Ugh.

"Well, I don't suppose you'll change much now," she said. "Barring a miracle or divine intervention."

I knew she blamed herself for our situation, but I was actually fine with it. Better than fine even, I told her. And it was true. I was fine. It was her I had to convince.

Words were my friends and my job was my girlfriend. One that didn't cost me a bunch of time, money, talk my ear off, or cause me emotional distress. Yup, I was just fine.

In fact, though I had chosen not to let her in on the secret, I had found a hobby quite a few years back. I wasn't just a prodigy with words, I was also pretty good with numbers. Very good.

I was especially good at being able to see trends and found checking the stock listings in the daily paper intriguing. It was almost like the numbers were jumping off the page at me. Organizing themselves in different colored categories in my brain. I was able to remember exactly where a particular stock had been a day, a week or a month prior and accurately predict future share price movements. To some, the stock pages looked like just a huge grey page full of numbers, but to me it looked like a simple mathematical equation: buy low now, sell high later.

As a 12-year-old, I'd set up an online trading account in my mom's name and began investing my newspaper delivery and lawn mowing money in a handful of stocks that looked good to me, including Pfizer, Apple and Microsoft. All had delivered in spades since then, paying my way to journalism school and allowing my mom to quit her full time job and work part time at a local senior's home. It made her happy to help people. And it made me happy to see her happy.
I'd since put some of the profits into crypto currencies, mostly Bitcoin, and was seeing some impressive returns. Into the six-figure range. I made sure to take a portion of the profits out periodically, just in case. I was NOT going to be one of those people who lost everything if the market crashed.
And I wasn't going to spend money like the proverbial drunken sailor, either.
We still lived in the same little two-story house, on the same street, in the same neighborhood. But it had a new white picket fence around the front yard, a newly shingled roof complete with solar panels, and a new paint job. I was able to do the fence and paint myself, but hired professionals for the hard stuff. Even with Mr. Google's help, I wasn't sure I wanted to install my own solar panels. Besides, I wasn't crazy about heights and two stories up looked pretty high to me.
 Inside, I treated mom to her dream kitchen renovation – she did more cooking now that she was only working part time, taking extra care not to let the meat, potatoes or rice and vegetables touch on my plate – new hardwood floors and some new furniture. It wasn't excessive, it wasn't exactly posh, but it was a nice little house that my mom could be proud of. And so was I.

Nope, money definitely isn't a problem. Work is good.
I'm doing just fine, Mom, thanks for asking.

Chapter 3 — Tessa

I'm a chatterbox. Always have been. Guilty as charged. I throw myself on the mercy of the court. I know it, but I can't help it. Whatever's in my brain just comes straight out my mouth.

My dad says I'm like a human Energizer Bunny – I just keep going, and going, and going. And talking, and talking, and talking. When I have no one to talk to, my inside voice (or should I say voices?) goes into overdrive, capable of carrying on multiple internal conversations at a time. Often, when driving, I arrive at my destination with no recollection of the route I've taken to get there – my mind having been lost in thought the entire time.

On the one hand, I reasoned, it didn't seem all that safe to be so out of it while behind the wheel. On the other hand, I was still alive, so … how bad could it be?

My mom, a clinical psychiatrist and one of more than 30,000 employees at the Mayo Clinic here in Rochester, says I have ADHD.

I like the Energizer Bunny analogy better.

And so, in keeping with my nature, on my way home from the interview, the process of mentally beating myself up began.

I usually have no idea how a job interview has gone. Of course, I'd only applied for part time fast food and retail positions in the past, but this was for sure the shortest – and strangest – interview I'd ever had. As I drove, I thought of all the things I could have done differently and decided just about everything. Grrr.

I'm filled with an overwhelming sense of relief as I pull up in front of our house, a nice bungalow in a nice suburb on the outskirts of the city.

In addition to being home to the world-famous Mayo Clinic, Rochester was also notable for being located in one of only four counties in Minnesota without a natural lake. This in the state whose license plate boasts 10,000 lakes. What are the odds? I thought, trying to do the math in my head and quickly giving up. Numbers weren't my thing.

I put the automatic transmission in my 2015 Ford Focus in park, shut off the ignition, unlocked my seatbelt ... and sat there. I need to steel myself for the onslaught of questions that is sure to come.

"Well, Freddy," I say out loud. "This is it."

I name all my vehicles, this one was Freddy the fabulous Ford Focus.

My dad liked to joke that Ford stood for Fix or Repair Daily, but I'd gotten five good years out of Freddy already. When I was away at Carleton, he was probably my best friend. Certainly the only one I'd probably see again once I went back home to the States. Yup, old Freddy and I had many one-sided heart-to-carburetor conversations driving back and forth to school, and then all the way home each summer. He was a great listener and, so far, had never let me down. The Rick Astley of cars, Freddy would never ever let me down.

I was an only child, and so the sole focus of my parents' expectations. Lucky me.

They're older parents – they didn't have me until they were nearly 40 – and just don't relate to, well, reality. Both were very busy with their careers in their 20s and early 30s.

"Far too busy to have children," my mom had once told me. Or too self-centered, I thought.

My dad tries to communicate by talking what he thinks is cool speak. Unfortunately, the last time Dad was cool, if ever, was in the '70s and what he thinks is far out and groovy just isn't cool anymore. Dig?

When I think about it, which I wish I didn't, but can't seem to control, I'm surprised they found the time to have a child at all. I wonder if they still, well, you know … did it. Yuk. I scrunch my face up at the thought.

I remember literally asking my mom why they were together – I blurt everything out, remember?

"He makes me laugh," she had replied without a moment's hesitation.

"Um, it doesn't look like you're laughing," I had pointed out to her. "Or sound like it."

"I'm laughing on the inside, dear," she had said. "Your dad knows. He's secure. He doesn't need any kind of external positive affirmation."

It's a good thing, I thought, because he sure doesn't get any from you. At least, not that I could see. Which only left... again... I don't want to know.

My mom is a clinical psychiatrist and her mannerisms are, well, clinical. She doesn't exactly give off a warm and fuzzy vibe. She isn't what you'd call a hugger. Yet here I am.

And Dad is still here too. For whatever reasons. Love?

So I give her the benefit of the doubt. So what if she didn't come to my high school ball games because she didn't like sports? She didn't see the point to them. So, what if she didn't watch cartoons and animated movies with Dad and I? I mean, we didn't watch online psychiatry seminars with her.

My dad did suggest once that maybe we could watch the Dr. Phil show as a family. "It has something for all of us," he'd suggested.

I'll never forget my mom's reaction. It was if someone had reached around her back and flipped a switch. She went ballistic. It was the first, and hopefully last, time I ever see her that emotional.

"Dr. Phil is NOT a real doctor!!" she exploded. "He just plays one on TV."

I didn't know Dr. Phil was such a sore spot for her, but somehow we had touched a nerve. A very sensitive nerve.

"Dr. Phil has a Ph. D. in Psychology," she informed us matter-of-factly. "He may call himself Dr., but he's no more a doctor than someone with a doctorate in English Literature is. He can't prescribe medication. He hasn't even renewed his license to practice psychology since 2006. In 2008 he was actually charged for practicing without a license in California for his 'treatment' of Brittany Spears. Dr. Phil indeed."

Whoa. So, my mom was not Dr. Phil's biggest fan. Good to know just in case ... in case what?

"Psychologists," she snorted derisively, "all talk and no action."

Which, technically, I suppose, was true. It was psychologists who had you lay down on a couch and asked, "Tell me about your childhood?" Psychiatrists were medical doctors who could prescribe drugs.

Dad and I agreed we'd watch Dr. Phil and maybe Oprah on the small TV in his workshop in the garage. It would be our little secret, he said.

My dad was a retired electrical engineer – hence the Tesla (and now Elon Musk) hero worship – he quit work at 55 with a full pension (whatever that meant, I wasn't great with numbers, remember) and now spent most of his time golfing, inventing things and making up lame dad jokes. Except that he didn't think they were lame.   He thought they were hilarious and I was his favorite audience. Make that captive audience.

We do have a similar sense of humor, no doubt from watching all those cartoons and videos together. We both know the words to every song in Disney's animated Beauty and the Beast and we love to quote lines from Toy Story to each other. "To infinity, and beyond!" I would state boldly as I left for high school each day.

Dad also did all the cooking and was pretty good at it, if you liked barbecue. He barbecued everything. The list of things he'd put on the barbecue reads like the list of things the Tasmanian Devil would eat on the old Bugs Bunny show. Aardvarks, ants, bears, boars, cats, bats, dogs, hogs, elephants, antelopes, pheasants, ferrets, giraffes, gazelles … basically, everything but the kitchen sink.

He'd even barbecue bacon by making a little tinfoil tray to contain the grease.

"It saves having to get the frying pan all dirty," he says. "But, Tessa, you must remember to never, ever, barbecue bacon while nude."

No duh.

"Cook bacon naked you must not," he repeats in what he thinks is his Yoda voice, from Star Wars, but which actually sounds to me more like Kermit the Frog from The Muppets. Setting the bad impressions and old movie references aside, I believe, technically, bacon is always nude. Unless the pig wore clothing while it was alive. I've heard the expression 'lipstick on a pig', but never clothing. I know what he meant, though, laugh and promise I'll at least wear an apron, which made him laugh. He laughed a lot.

I can't see myself ever having a good reason to barbecue bacon naked, even without the sage advice.

As expected, they're both waiting for me in the living room as I walk in the door. Dad in plaid golf shorts and a Pink Floyd Dark Side of the Moon T-shirt, Mom in a severe-looking pantsuit (think a rail-thin Hilary Clinton). But at least she was here.

"So ...", says my mom.

"How did it go?" finishes my dad.

Hmm. They finished each other's sentences. Maybe there IS something there? Somewhere, under all those layers of bad jokes and tacky pant suits.

"Okay, I guess. I really don't know. The guy who interviewed me, Mr. Osborne, he's a pretty hard guy to read."

I went on to describe the interview and, as I ramble on, it strikes me that I didn't really screwed it up that bad. He'd never really given me the time to answer anything, to talk, and maybe that was a good thing? Maybe I'd have talked myself right out of it. He didn't seem like the type who cared much for small talk, chit chat or bafflegab. All of which were my specialties.

"Classic insecure alpha male behavior," snips my mom. "The human equivalent of peeing around his territory. I don't like him."

"Did his office smell funny?" asks my dad.

To which my mom responds with an eye-roll and sticking her nose back in her book, On Human Nature by Edward O. Wilson.

Oh great, I think, I can hardly wait to have HIS theories applied to my life.

Thinking back, Mr. Osborne's office DID smell funny. I was willing to bet, however, that it was his cologne – and not urine.

"Anyways," I continue, "I have to have my best written piece and my best news podcast on his desk, well, on his secretary's email by 9 a.m. tomorrow."

"Secretary?"

I've got my mom's attention again.

"What a Neanderthal."

"Excellent!" exclaims my dad, "that means you've got a great shot at it. You know," he says to me, "Wayne Gretzky said 'you miss 100% of the shots you don't take'."

Wayne Gretzky, the great one, arguably the best hockey player to ever live. Minnesota was known as a hockey state. EVERYONE has heard of Gretzky.

True dat, I think. I'll take my best shot, alright. But I'm a ball player, not a hockey fan, so I'll hit this one out of the park. A grand slam.

This was a chance to start a career. A new life. To reinvent myself as whoever and whatever I wanted to be. No more high school or college cliques. No cool kids or mean girls. Just grown adults working together as colleagues to achieve a common goal.

I wasn't underestimating this opportunity. It was way more to me than just a job. Right now, it was everything. My hopes, my dreams ... my ticket out of this town. To bigger and better things.

I'd submit my best stuff, alright. Prepare to be blown away, Mr. Osborne!

Chapter 4 — Tessa

"Congratulations!" the voice on the other end of my iPhone says. No, sings. "You've got the internship."

"Um, thanks," I stammer, not quite sure who I'm talking to.

"You don't recognize me, do you?"

"Well, we ARE on the phone. I'm sorry, I don't recognize your voice, but I'm guessing you're from the Star-Bulletin's HR department."

"Close. It's Suzi Kwan, Mr. Osborne's executive assistant."

"Oh sure, hi Suzi. Thanks for calling."

"You STILL don't recognize me, do you? From Woodside High? I live in Arborfield. You were probably too busy hitting home runs and stuff. I was the quiet Chinese girl."

I remember her now. There weren't many Asians in our high school. Plenty of blue-eyed blondes, this IS Minnesota, after all, with many folks of Scandinavian descent. Besides, she looks VERY different now. I hadn't noticed her before, but I did now – which was, of course, what her unique rockabilly look was all about. She'd reinvented herself after high school.

Unfortunately, I haven't. Yet. I'm kind of short at 5'1". Not much I can do about that, despite what I'd told that old baseball coach. And I don't like wearing heels.

I'm maybe a bit of a chunky monkey at a healthy and happy 130 pounds, a good portion of that in the old caboose. I was fine with it. I filled out a pair of jeans nicely, in my opinion. Besides, wasn't that the look these days? A little junk in the trunk?

When I stop to think about it, there isn't anything really memorable about me, unless you've seen me play ball. I'm very … average, bordering on tomboyish. I usually wear jeans and T-shirts, with my straight, shoulder-length mousy-brown hair pulled back in a short ponytail. I didn't really have a 'look', I just – am.

"I yam what I yam", my dad would say in his best Popeye the Sailor voice.

My mom isn't crazy about Popeye because he has tattoos and smokes a pipe. She can be a bit judgy that way.

"Sure," I say. "I remember you now. "Don't your parents own the Wok Inn restaurant on Woodside Drive?"

"Yup," she chimes quite cheerily, "that's us. Let me know next time you order take-out and I'll get you a discount."

"Sounds good," I say. "I can't remember the last time we ate Chinese. Food. Chinese food. My dad likes to barbecue. If you can't barbecue it, we don't eat it."

The sound of Suzi's laughter erupts over the phone.

"Too freaking funny!" she half shouts. "My dad only deep fries. Everything. Except maybe rice. You'll have to invite me to dinner sometime."

Wow, I think, this gal's no shrinking violet! I've only really just met her and she's inviting herself over for dinner. She doesn't know what she's getting herself into.

"Ya, sure", I say, suddenly realizing I was saying that quite a bit. Maybe too much.

"Anyhow," she sings out. "I was wondering if I could catch a ride with you in the morning. You know, since we live so close. I've been taking transit, but it takes so long and I have to get a transfer to go downtown and it's so crowded and in winter it can be cold waiting at the stop. My dad goes in to work early, so he can drop me at your place around 7:45 if that's okay? I can give you gas money."

And I thought I was a fast talker. I have nothing on Suzi.

"Ya, sure," I say, again. Then quickly adding, before she can speak, "If you don't mind my asking, which of the work samples I submitted got me the job?"

I wondered if it was the serious news article I'd written on the near-epidemic level of prescription drug abuse by students, especially around exam time, for the campus newspaper? Or the tongue in cheek podcast I'd posted on the newspaper's online edition investigating the overnight appearance of Mickey Mouse faces in hundreds of clocks around the university. With a bit of digging, I'd been able to discover the identities of some of the culprits and, while I agreed not to name names, I did name the department they came from – Engineering.

My dad had just grinned when I told him. He WAS an engineer. He'd been an engineering student. That grin … it seemed like he wanted to say something but was holding back. Probably for the best. I don't need to know all my dad's secrets.

"Neither," says Suzi, with what seems like way too much certainty. "You were the only one to make deadline."

This news, while good, does absolutely nothing to alleviate my self-doubt as a writer. It was one thing at the university level, but J school was still just that, school. I still have no idea how I stack up in the 'real' world, or what Mr. Osborne thinks of my work.

"You report to Steve Sondergaard in City at 9 a.m. Monday. I'll see you at your place at quarter to eight. Later gator!"

And with that she's gone. Like a genie. Poof! She popped in, granted my wish, and popped out again. Hmm, I think, I wonder if I get two more wishes? And if I do, what should they be? For now, I decide, opening my closet and looking at the slim pickings that represent my entire 'wardrobe, I'd settle for some fashion advice. For that, though, I wasn't asking Suzi.

I decided on a pair of black slacks with a white unisex dress shirt and red blazer. No, not red. Red's too bold, it's more subtle than that, a little more … magenta. I was just putting it on and grabbing my shoes when the doorbell rings. It's only 7:39. Lucky for me, I had trouble sleeping and woke up early. Yup, lucky me.

"Hey," I say, answering the door. No doubt impressing her with my magnificent command of the English language.

"Good morning!" she sings out melodiously. "What a beautiful day! Sorry I'm a bit early. My dad says if you're not five minutes early, you're late."

I need a coffee. Badly. Extra sugar.

"My car's out in the garage," I say, filling my 'to go' cup and heading for the door. "My dad's out there in his workshop, he calls it his time machine. He's harmless, just ignore him."

"Hey Tessa!" gushes my dad, overenthusiastically, as usual, as we enter, pausing momentarily from his morning workout. Curls for girls, he likes to say. What girls, I don't know. Mom?

"And …"

"Suzi", interjects Suzi. "I work with Tessa at the S-B."

"Suzi!" he practically yells. "Welcome to the '80s." He gestures with his arms.

"S-B? Are you sure you don't mean B-S?"

He laughs at his own joke. So lame.

"Star-Bulletin," says Suzi. "Sorry, I tend to slip into text speak once in a while."

"NP," says my dad, giving the thumbs up sign. Also the secret signal for me to roll my eyes.

"You girls come for the gun show," he says, jokingly, I hope, as he does a mock pose-down, flexing his biceps – which are not as big as he thinks.

KMN, I think, glancing over at Suzi. I'll bet that's what she's thinking. At this rate, I'd have eye strain before I even sat down to the computer at work. I might as well go into permanent eye roll mode, I think, and just roll them forward every now and again when he's NOT embarrassing me. Or maybe start wearing sunglasses everywhere, like Bono from U2 or Roy Orbison.

My future's so bright I need to wear shades.

Suzi, for her part, seems unfazed.

"You should probably get those things registered Mr. T. You know, before you get arrested for carrying a concealed weapon or something."

"I pity the fool that messes with me," growls my dad, imitating the real Mr. T, an aging tough-guy movie and TV star.

I instinctively roll my eyes. Again. At least I hope it was instinct. Either that or, gasp, I'm turning into my mother. My worst fears realized. Okay, not worst, but right up there.

"Have a great day girls," he says jovially, unscathed, preening and smoothing his dark brown hair in the mirror as we turn to leave, no doubt contemplating how he'd look in a Mohawk haircut and cluster of heavy gold chains.

"I like your dad," says Suzi as we climb into my car. "He's funny."

"I'm sure he likes you too. He likes anyone who laughs at his jokes."

She giggles.

Other people always seem to think my dad is funny. I don't
see it, but, then, I've probably just been exposed to his
'humor' too long.

"My parents don't speak English. I have to tell them when
stuff is funny. They'd love your dad. Speaking of jokes," she
continues, not stopping to breathe, "about your new boss,
Steve ... he's a bit of a Richard."

I must look like I don't understand, so she begins to
elaborate.

"A dick. A jerk. An a..."

"Okay," I say slowly, "good to know."

What had I got myself into?

"They call him mini Oz because he's just like big Oz. He even
combs his eyebrows the same."

Bit of a jerk, I thought, and this coming from the person who
works for Mr. Osborne! This should be interesting, I mean,
how bad could it be? And what's with the eyebrows? I
ponder, remembering Mr. Osborne's own owl-like forehead
whiskers. A good pair of hedge trimmers was in order, for
sure.

I'd seen some bad comb-overs in my time, but combing your
eyebrows up to, what, hide your forehead wrinkles? That
was a new one for me. Or was it to deliberately look like an
owl in an odd – very odd – attempt to look 'wise'? Was this
Steve guy another grumpy old fart like Osborne?

I wondered what my mom would think. And then just as
quickly regretted it. No, I don't, I thought. I'll make up my
own mind this time, thank you very much.

"Here we are," squeals Suzi. Honestly, I've never seen
anyone so excited to arrive at work in the morning. "Park
over there," pointing to a spot away from the other vehicles
and popping open her purse.

As soon as I put Freddy into park, she snaps open a Tupperware container and begins de-piercing. Well, you can't really de-pierce yourself, I guess, but she carefully removes her facial piercings before we head in to the office. First the eyebrow barbell, then the nose ring – the multiple ear studs stay in, mostly hidden by her shoulder-length Paige-boy haircut.

"Ta da!" she calls out like a Vegas magician. "I have more piercings," she says, noticing me noticing her. "But you can't see them. At least not right now."

I blush. She laughs.

We're early, and I'm nervous. No, excited, about my first day. Thanks for the positive energy boost, Suzi! Driving to work with her was as good as having a second cup of coffee. I'm pumped!

"I've forwarded your work samples to Steve," she says merrily, "but you'll have to copy your resume. The copier room is down the hall and to your right. The coffee room is on the left."

"Thanks," I say, turning to head the opposite direction as Suzi heads for her post on guard outside Mr. Osborne's lair. Was she there to keep the dragon in or people out? I wonder.

"See you later."

"TTYL," says Suzi.

***

I'm fairly tech savvy. I can do your basic social media updates, post to YouTube and TikTok and even update websites on WordPress. But copy machines, they're a different animal all together. I laugh out loud as I recall Mr. Osborne interrupting our interview – was that an interview? I still wasn't quite sure it qualified, but whatever – to ask Suzi to 'Photostat' something. Yes, he had actually said 'Photostat'.

As I round the corner to the photocopy room, I notice there's already a young guy standing at the machine. Had he heard me laugh out loud to myself? Oh well, who cares? He looks like he's just another young worker like me. Maybe even another intern in a different department.

Kind of an 'interesting' look for a person, though – corduroy pants, striped shirt with plain white collar, sweater vest and, yes, that was a polka dot bowtie. I know some journalists are nerds, but this was ridiculous. I'd heard in J school that's how it was. The newsroom was the traditional bastion of the intelligence, the smart people, otherwise known as 'nerd central'.

The advertising sales department, at the far end of the hall, was where the cool kids hung out. They were better looking, in general, or thought they were, and were more aggressive, bordering, I'd been told, on outright obnoxious. It was a fine line, I suppose.

The two departments were at opposite ends of the building for a reason and it was unusual to see members of one department or the other venture into the other's territory. This dude at the copier was definitely NOT in advertising. He looks like the dorkiest of dorks, giving me the confidence to speak up.

"Hi. I'm Tessa."

"Hi," bowtie guy mutters, not looking up from the paper jam he's fixing. He has a baby face and round, wire-rimmed John Lennon-style glasses.

Hmm. Not much of a conversationalist, probably just shy, being such a dork and all.

"There," he says, "all fixed."

"Thanks", I say. "I'm a new intern. It's my first day and I'm supposed to copy my resume for my supervisor, Steve. I hear he's a bit of a jerk, so I don't want to be late."

I slipped my resume into the feeder tray as I spoke. If there's one skill I HAVE mastered, it's being able to keep talking while doing basically anything. Yup, I'm a real verbal multi-tasked.

"Hey!"

My resume copy shot out and Bowtie guy grabbed it – and…was…reading it.

"Excuse me", I say in what I hope is a calm but firm tone. "Can I …"

"Hi," he says again, still reading.

Ya, ya, geek boy, we've covered the 'hi' thing already. Now give me back my resume.

"I'm the jerk. But you can just call me Steve. Follow me."

Oops. Ouch!

Now THIS is embarrassing. Far more embarrassing than the gun show incident with my dad and Suzi this morning. More embarrassing even than the time we went to the Mayan Riviera in Mexico and my dad came out of the hotel wearing a microscopic Speedo. Yup, my dear old dad, rocking the canary yellow banana hammock. With a strategically-placed happy face on it no less! For a brief moment I was tempted to remove my sunglasses and stare directly at the tropical sun in an attempt to sear the image from my brain.

My mom must have noticed the pained expression on my face, because she leaned over to me on her lawn chair and whispered "It could have been worse, Tessa. He was looking at man thongs when I left him in the swimwear department."

"What are you girls whispering about?" queried my dad, jogging up to us, his man parts bouncing to and fro freely, unrestrained. Please don't, I thought. Closing my eyes behind my glasses.

"Oh just what nice buns you have dear," lied my mom turning and giving me a shrug, as if to say 'whatever'.

And then to me, "It won't look so bad once he goes in the cold water."

With that she went back to reading her book. I can't see the title, but it's by Life Coach Mike Bayer, a frequent guest on Dr. Phil and one of the people my mother loves to hate for no good reason. Sometimes I think she's just jealous they're on TV and she's not. I know she'd say that was nonsense, but still, I wonder …

"Tessa?"

It's Steve, startling me out of my reverie, motioning me to follow him. He's not smiling.

This is not starting out well.

Chapter 5 — Steve

 "Hi," I say, my voice and face as stern as I can muster.
"I'm the jerk. But you can just call me Steve. Follow me."
 In truth, I'm chuckling on the inside. I enjoy making the
newbie's squirm and this one is going to be fun.
Ah, there it is, the deer in the headlights look I love so much.
Just standing there. Staring blankly, straight ahead, at my …
bowtie? Perhaps she's mesmerized by the polka dots. Could
happen. Like the snake's eyes in that terrifying Jungle Book
movie my mom made me watch when I was little in an
attempt to get me to like cartoons. She never tried that stunt
again.
"Tessa?" I say, motioning to follow me.
I can tell she doesn't know what to say, so I say nothing.
What would she say if she could? What could you say after
you'd just stuck your foot in your mouth so completely?
Not much. So I let her stew in the juices of her own silence
for another minute.
One full minute. I time it as I pretend to read her resume.
There was a psychological need for people to fill the void
silence creates, I know. It's an old interviewing trick I learned
from Mr. Osborne and it works as well with employees as it
does with politicians. People care unable to resist the urge to
speak, to fill the void, with something, anything. Silence is
unnerving. And this is precisely where they often say
something they'd later regret. Which, of course, if you're a
journalist, is great.
I wonder if she'll make that classic blunder and put her other
foot in her mouth too. I'm more than willing to give her
enough rope. I'm a patient man, or so I keep telling myself.

"So," I say, too loudly, deliberately, to startle her, throw her on the defensive, "I'll let you in on a little secret," I lean forward and whisper … "it's true."

"W-What's true?" she says, hesitantly, still taken aback by my full frontal assault and trying vainly to pry her foot back out of her mouth without the aid of pliers.

There's no toolbox around here, little girl. The only hardware here is in my computer. You'll have to think your way out of this one. She's just a little minute of a thing. I wonder if she has the jam to be a reporter. Well, we were about to find out.

"I can be a bit of a jerk," I say. "I don't mean to be. I'm just very … direct. I don't like to waste words and I don't like to waste time. I'm not here to be your friend and I don't care if you like me. We're here to do a job and I need people who can do that. If I have to babysit you, I can't use you. If you can't bring something to the team that no one else does, I can't use you. If I can't count on you, Tessa, I can't use you. Can I count on you, Tessa?"

She still hasn't said a word. Not good. I want, no, need, people who can stand up for themselves. People who can give as well as they can take, especially when it came to covering the politicos down at City Hall. You really had to cut through the crap and pin those clowns down. If they smelled weakness, blood in the water, you were toast.

My job, as I see it, is to weed out the riff raff. To make it as difficult as possible for the interns so that only the truly worthy are left standing in the end. An internship at the Star-Bulletin wasn't an automatic guarantee of a job at the end of the three-month term. It was an audition, and the director, me, was a stickler for attention to detail. In fact, with my eyebrows combed up like Mr. Osborne, I fancied I looked a little like a young Martin Scorsese, the famous movie director.

Besides, just a few months shy of my 21st birthday, it was still the only facial hair I could grow.

Sink or swim. Throw them in the deep end of the pool and see what happens.

That's what Mr. Osborne had done with me. The difference was, that when Mr. Osborn hired me I was 18 going on 35. I'd basically been an adult living in a child's body since I was about eight. The past few interns that had come my way had been total morons with a sense of entitlement big enough to sink the Titanic.

Plus, they, like, had, like, a problem, like, communicating clearly. I remember one young gal, her grades were great, but how could I possibly send her out to interview someone? Such a ditz. She'd NEVER be able to actually write an article – and that's what I need. A full-fledged journalist, not a wanna-be whose 'best' years were already behind them at their high school yearbook or college paper.

I want grownups, not kids. I want someone like me … and Mr. Osborne.

I'm willing to throw them a live saver in the form of mentorship – just like Mr. Osborne did for me – if they have potential and the common sense to ask for help, but so far no one has asked.

"I'm sorry," she says, finally. "I'm just really nervous."

You can say that again.

"And when I'm nervous I talk too much."

And that. But at least she's honest. Very honest. Personal integrity is a good thing in a journalist, or anyone for that matter.

"Yes."

"Yes, what?" I reply, looking her deep in her eyes. Were they green? Or more of a grey? "Yes, I'm a jerk or yes, I can count on you?"

"Yes, you can count on me. 110%. I really, really, really want a career in journalism. Hopefully one day cover sports."

"Sports," I say.

So I had myself a jock here. A muscle head who thought they could write about sports just because they could kick or throw a ball. Well, I'd soon see about that. Interning in City was a long way from Sports, especially for a young woman. It wasn't fair, I knew, but it was what it was.

"Alright then," I fairly shout, startling her again. This was so much fun!

"That's what I want to hear."

It wasn't. I wanted her to say … what? I'm not sure what I wanted her to say. Anything, really, to show she couldn't be intimidated because, as Dorothy said in the Wizard of Oz: "Toto, I've a feeling we're not in Kansas anymore."

I didn't much care for movies, but I'd been compelled to watch it once I heard the Oz reference applied to Mr. Osborne. I found I could relate to the Tin Man. I liked him. He was a no-nonsense, get things done, don't let your emotions get in the way kind of guy. My kind of guy.

I'd also watched one episode of Dr. Oz on TV, but it wasn't the same at all.

Nope, this wasn't high school or college. This wasn't amateur hour. This wasn't some silly reality show. This was the real thing. The big leagues. This was for serious journalists only.

I watch her as I read out the job description and expectations, looking for some clue to her reaction in her facial expressions or body language.

The main duties of an intern include writing obituary notices (known as obits in the news game), fact checking advertorials for the feature department and proof reading whatever was put in front of you.

Most people don't realize we have people here do the obits, but it was a necessary evil if you wanted them to be written decently. It was also a great way to humble cocky young interns who thought they were going to break the next Watergate or Iran Contra scandal.

She stops taking notes and looks up.

"Sweet!" she says, almost too enthusiastically.

Does she actually WANT to write obits? Nobody does, really.

"Any questions?"

"Just one, okay, two. One, what's an advertorial? And, two, will I have a chance to cover sports at all?"

Great, a sign of life, she asked for what she wants.

I know from having to fend for myself from an early age that sometimes in life, no, most of the time, you have to ask for what you want. People aren't going around knocking on doors giving away jobs on silver platters. If you want it, you have to ask for it, and then work hard to keep it. She has goals ... and that's good. A lot of people her age don't. Maybe there IS some potential there. Maybe.

"An advertorial is an article that an advertising client has paid for. We write a story on their business or product, they proof it, and we run what they want with a little tag on it identifying it as an 'Ad Feature'. Never lie to your readers, Tessa. If its ad copy, tell them. If our readers can't trust us, we're done.

"As for covering sports, only if a local athlete dies. For now, check in with Suzi. She'll show you to your desk and get you set up on email and such. She'll also introduce you to the

Features editor and show you where to find your work assignments on Trello. You are familiar with Tello, aren't you? And Google Docs?"

"Sure," she replies, a little too quickly for my liking.

Oh well, we'll find out soon enough. I wonder if Mr. Osborne has any other resumes handy. Just in case.

So, I think, as she walks out of my office, they think I'm a jerk, do they? It's a good thing I don't care. I know I wasn't going to win any popularity contests, or be nominated to head-up the company social committee, but I didn't know it was THAT bad.

Tough but fair, I could live with. But jerk?

Hmm. I straighten my bowtie. A ritual I perform multiple times daily.

Other than the jerk part, that went pretty well.

Chapter 6 — Tessa

That. Did. Not. Go. Well.

I think.

Or maybe say out loud to myself.

I'm not sure anymore what I've thought and what I've said, I'm so flustered right now.

Sinking into the warm embrace of Freddy's well-worn interior is like slipping back into the womb. Okay, maybe not quite that safe and secure, or painful, probably, but my car is definitely my happy place. I shudder involuntarily at what my mom would say if she ever heard me say that.

That, I vow, is something I'll have to keep to my inside voice only.

I'd covered the vinyl seats, in the front anyways, with nice fluffy seat covers. If you've ever climbed into a car with plastic seats on a cold Minnesota winter morning you'll understand why. Nothing – and I do mean nothing – ever happened in the back seat, so I left it to fade and crack with the sun and cold summer/winter cycles. I covered the steering wheel in the same fluffy material. Nothing was too good for my Freddy. Except maybe regular oil changes. I'm not too good at remembering those.

"Obits, Freddy," I say, this time out loud for sure. "Obits. Freaking obits!"

You couldn't interview dead people, obviously, so that meant speaking with their survivors to get the details of their loved one's life. I'd only been to two funerals in my entire life, my mom's parents a few years back, a year apart, in Duluth. Now I had to do it every day. I didn't have to go to the funerals, but I did have to contact the people who had purchased obituaries and make sure they were written properly and fact-checked to death. A very apt description, I thought. Pun intended.

What IS news to me (I'm really getting good at this pun thing), is that you actually have to pay to run an obituary. I always thought the paper just ran them as a kind of courtesy tribute. The more public the figure, the bigger the tribute. But, as is so often the case in life, as it turns out, you get what you pay for.

They didn't teach you that in J school. In fact, thinking back, they didn't teach me ANYTHING about the BUSINESS of the news. After all, it was a business, not a free service. They were in the news biz to make money not – as the J school instructors would have you believe – to preserve the sanctity of truth, justice and the American constitution.

Which brings me to another part of my job, ad features, and the ultimate sell-out of one's journalistic integrity. The way they talked about it in J school, you'd think we were writing propaganda for the Nazis. In reality, how bad can it be? You just interview business people and say nice things about their company's product or service. Sure, it's promotional copy, but your names not on it, so what's the harm? Plus, you make lots of great contacts. Of course, I wasn't writing them, just calling to get the facts straight and stories approved. Nope, advertorials wouldn't be a problem for me. Same for the proof reading. I can read with the best of them, bring it on!

The tricky part is going to be the special assignment. An enterprise story. An Enterpriser was a story that no one assigned to you, one that you found on your own. And going to a movie, concert or ball game and writing a review wasn't going to cut it. Not like it had in high school or college. Nope, they wanted something with some bite. Some factual muscle. Some steak with the sizzle. Given my age, the fact I've been out of town at school for the past four years, and my business associates consist of former coworkers at McDonalds and a shoe store at the local mall – my contacts, and therefore idea sources, are somewhat limited.

"That's okay, Freddy," I say, pulling up to my home and pushing the garage door opener. "We'll come up with something."

Soon, I hope.

***

Mom and Dad are already sitting down to dinner when I walk in – barbecued pork back ribs, corn on the cob and green beans. Flatulence city.

"How did your first day go dear," asks my mom, before I've even closed the door or set down my purse.

"Great!" I yell, maybe a little too loudly. I dial it back a notch. "I called my boss a jerk and I'm sure he hates me."

"Oops. Ouch!" says my dad, echoing my earlier sentiments. I'm so much like him it's scary.

"Well I'm sure he deserved it dear," my mom says with her usual self-assuredness. In her mind, she's never wrong.

"Probably good for his self-awareness. The famous social psychologist George Herbert Mead called it 'looking glass self'. The ability to see oneself how others see you. Most people see what they want to see when they look in the mirror. It's not so easy to admit to what other people might be seeing."

Mmmm, ya, I think, I guess that makes sense. Although all I ever saw in the mirror was my own reflection, in all my plain-Jane glory. I half-hoped to see no reflection, meaning I was a vampire. At least then my life's purpose would be clear. Oh well, better to see things as they really are than to fool oneself into seeing something that's not there. Like they do with the mirrors at the ladies fashion boutiques. You know, the ones that make you look thinner.

"And then there's this girl," I say, "Anna. Anna Nordstrom. She wants to cover sports too and has a year's experience on me."

"I pity the fool who gets in your way," my dad growls, seemingly still in his Mr. T phase. He'd grow out of it. My mom rolled her eyes and my thoughts drift back to the office and Anna's grand entrance that morning.

* * *

The sounds a bustling newsroom makes have changed a lot over the last twenty years or so. Gone is the clickety-clack of fingers hammering away on manual or electric typewriters, replaced by the quieter keystrokes of the computer. Macs in the newsroom, graphic design and production departments. Cheaper PCs in the advertising, circulation and accounting areas. Each department still has a main landline, however, and every so often the shrill old-fashioned ring shrieks like a baby's cry in the night. I think I even saw it wake Morty, the Features editor, up from an afternoon siesta at his desk one day.

So the noises are different now, but there are still noises. That's what catches my attention that first morning. All of the noise … just … stopped. As they say in the movies, it was quiet, too quiet.

I look up from my computer, and there she is. Anna Nordstrom. The one and only. She'd just walked in the door and all eyes were on her – men, women and anyone in between. She's wearing, no, rocking, a bright red skirt with matching blazer, sheer black blouse with black push-up bra visible underneath and black pumps. There's no denying it. She. Is. Hot.

And she knows it.

So hot. Too hot for words. I imagined myself writing her obituary. What was THAT all about?

"It's all fake," Suzi had sidled up to me. "Boobs, lips, hair, butt, accent ..."

"Accent?" The boobs, sure, they were ... perfect. The bee-stung lips, the platinum blonde hair, that made sense too, but the accent?

"Ya," says Suzi. "She totally puts on that Southern drawl thing. I've seen her HR records. She's from Seattle."

"Seattle," I repeat, watching Anna's tight, toned buttocks swishing down the hall in her short skirt. I hoped I wouldn't have to compete with THAT my whole career.

I'd already lost the chance to host a weekly college podcast to a tall blonde a couple of years ago. I like to blame it on the huge zit I had on my chin the day of the auditions, but I knew, deep down, in my heart of hearts, that it was because she was a tall blonde and I ... wasn't.

Thank you, Karma, for the timing. The zit didn't leave a mark, but losing the podcast sure did.

I was determined not to let anything like that happen again. Ever.

A few weeks go by, and I'm settling in just fine, in my opinion.

One thing about writing obits, there's job security. And, I'm getting better at it. Not just the writing, but the dealing with the sad people part too. The fact checking and proof reading is going fine. Boring, but fine.

I even have an idea for my enterpriser!

My mom mentioned, one evening, over barbecued alligator (not as easy to get in Minnesota as you might think) and collard greens – it was Louisiana night, apparently – that researchers had made some kind of breakthrough in the treatment of MS. Not a cure, but something significant. She didn't know exactly what, but had given me a name and phone number, which I quickly emailed to my work address so I would have it when I need it.

Meanwhile, I'm really enjoying riding to work with Suzi. Her seemingly limitless supply of positive energy, she calls it 'Chi', is contagious. I find myself arriving to work happy every day and, maybe because of that, people are starting to notice me. In a good way.

Especially this one guy in the graphics department. I walk by his work station every morning and he's always got a smile and a warm "Good morning" for me. Not to mention he's tall, dark and super-talented. His name is Mickey, and he reminds me of the song, not the mouse. I even added it to my playlist and sometimes sing along when I'm driving. I don't know if it makes Freddy jealous or not.

"Hey Mickey," I usually say back.

So fine indeed. With work under control, perhaps I have time for a … distraction. Preferably of the tall, strong and silent variety.

Suzi likes our ride sharing deal too. Or at least she says so. No, I'm pretty sure she does.

She genuinely loves to see what my dad's working on, which makes her a very unique individual and a very welcome visitor to our home. She even chided me for not inviting her over for alligator.

Right now, Dad's big invention is a traceable golf ball. It emits a shrill beep, like a smoke detector alarm, presumably so a person can easily find it – not just to annoy the other golfers.

"You should totally build an App for that Mr. T," says Suzi, encouragingly, one day. "That way people can track it on their phone's GPS without anyone knowing they're cheating. Er, I mean, without bothering them with the noise," she semi-corrected herself, tongue clearly in cheek.

My dad has always said:"If you're not cheating, you're not trying hard enough."

And so I had cheated. Just a little. And only at baseball. Well, not cheated, exactly, just played hard. Put it this way, if you were between me and home plate, it probably wasn't going to go well for you.

"I'm also working on a remote control model with a tiny gyroscope built-in," he bragged shamelessly. "It gives a whole new meaning to driving the ball! Get it?"

"Ya, Dad, we got it," I say, making a huge effort not to roll my eyes. That's my mom's 'thing', and I'd like to keep it that way.

"Keep up the good work, Mr. T!" Suzi giggles. "You should go on Shark Tank."

"Don't give him any ideas," I tell her as we leave.

I like Suzi, but I sometimes wish I had someone other than her to do things with. Things like fishing, playing catch, camping. A guy friend would be nice. A boyfriend would be even better.

***

And then IT happened. And everything changed.

On my one-month anniversary on the job, I'm sitting at my desk, minding my own business, when a bouquet of flowers arrives. A beautiful bouquet. Not roses, but a lovely arrangement with lots of color. I see the delivery guy arrive, holding the bouquet, and head straight to Anna's desk. She gets flowers all the time, so he assumes they're for her. Today, however, they're not for her.

"Oh Tessa!" she calls my voice out across the newsroom. "Flowers for you." She's far too cheerful about it as she gets up and swishes her perfect bum over to my desk.

"Someone's got a secret admirer," she announces for all to hear. She'd probably been a great Happy Birthday singer at the Cheesecake Factory in a past life. "Or a boyfriend," she finishes, snatching the attached card from the bouquet and reading it out loud.

"Happy one-month anniversary. Signed, M. Oooh," she says, chanting like a 7th grader, "Tessa's got a boyfriend. Tessa's got a boyfriend."

I feel myself blushing so much I worry my head might literally explode. If it does, I hope I take her out with me. But then who will write our obits? Get your head together, Tessa.

The message was from my mom. That's what the M stood for and I'd recognize her handwriting anywhere. She's a doctor, right?

But the damage is done. I'm either going to have to admit my mommy sent me flowers, or come up with a boyfriend. Quick. One whose name starts with an M.

I glanced across the room to where Mickey is working, a look of concentration on his ruggedly handsome face as he puts tomorrow's front page together. Hmm, I wonder …

Later, near the end of the day, so I can beat a hasty retreat if necessary, I saunter casually over to Mickey's desk. My heart is pounding. Thank goodness he has ear buds in, or he'd hear it for sure.

Thump, thump. Thump, thump.

"Hey, Mickey," I say, waving my hand in greeting. Please, God, don't let the next words out of my mouth be 'You're so fine'.

"Hi Tessa," he says, popping out the ear bud nearest me. One thing about my generation, we'll have no trouble adapting to wearing hearing aids.

"Nice flowers. What's up?"

"They're from my mom," I say. "Please don't tell anyone."

"No worries," he laughs easily. "Your secret's safe with me." Such a good guy.

"Anyways," I say, gathering up all the courage I can muster. Was this what it was like for guys? This was brutal. "I was wondering if you maybe wanted to, um, go to the Rochester Red Wings baseball game tomorrow night?"

The Red Wings were the Triple A minor league affiliate of the Washington Nationals, and it was pretty good baseball.

"Oh, Tessa," a frown forms on his chiseled face. "I'm sorry. I'm gay. I thought everybody knew."

Everybody but me, apparently. It figures. Tall, good looking. Nice. Artistic. I should have been able to read between the lines. He checked all the boxes except one. A very important one. Crap.

I try not to let my disappoint show on my face, not sure if I'm succeeding – probably not – and tried to think of what to say next.

"Um, oh, uh, okay. Sorry. See you tomorrow."

Sorry?! What was I sorry for? That he couldn't go? That he was gay? Both?

Unless I came clean about the flowers, I was going to need a boyfriend. Fast.

Oh well, I thought while rinsing my coffee cup in the break room, maybe I'll meet someone at the company slow pitch tournament.

I signed my name at the bottom of the sheet on the bulletin board, went back to my desk to open up my Mayo Clinic story on my computer and … it was gone!

Chapter 8 — Steve

Things are going well for me at work.

The new intern, Tessa, is fitting in well. She has a natural knack for writing obits. They aren't as easy as people think, what with having to deal with input from several different family members, all of whom believe they are best-selling authors waiting to be discovered and who want to approve every single word of the final version.

They usually complain about the price too, even though that has nothing to do with the Editorial department.

There's a huge divide between Advertising and Editorial, between church and state, that isn't common knowledge to the outside world. Within the walls of the newspaper, however, it might as well be an invisible Great Wall of China. As far as building fences went, Donald Trump has nothing on the employees at the Bulletin-Star.

Even advertorials are easier. At least they only require one person's approval.

Nope, work's going well. Boring, almost.

It's at home where things are getting … weird.

Something's happening to my mom. I'd heard about the 'M' word, menopause, 'the change', and the things it could do to women, both physically and emotionally. It wasn't her MS, I was pretty sure – that's been stable for a while now, but something is definitely going on with her. Something I don't fully understand.

It was about to become clear. Crystal clear.

***

"I'm worried about you, dear," my mom says, closing her laptop.

I'm in the kitchen, folding laundry I've just brought up from the dryer downstairs. As well as my mom's doing health-wise, she doesn't handle stairs well.

"I'm fine, Mom," I say, and I am. I think. As far as I know. Other than that 'jerk' comment which, for some reason, I can't erase from my brain. Delete. Delete. Delete.

"You don't go out enough," she yells. "You need some friends, a hobby, a girlfriend. I wouldn't mind being a grandma, you know. Lord knows I'm not going to live forever."

This again.

"I've got my work, Mom, and the work around here, and I DO have a hobby, investing, remember?"

"Investing. There you go with that investing again. How do you meet people investing online?"

She seems oblivious to the fact it's my investing that allowed us to renovate our home and, in fact, I actually paid out the mortgage last year. Unbeknownst to her.

I'd looked into some of the higher-end care facilities for her, but after visiting a couple I just couldn't see myself shipping her off, like unwanted goods, to become someone else's problem. I would do whatever I had to keep her in her home, our home, for as long as possible.

"Anyways," she goes on, "speaking of meeting people online …"

I didn't know we were, and the hairs on the back of my neck were starting to tingle. I don't like where this was going. She's online dating. My mom is looking for men on the Internet. My stomach feels queasy. I gag and throw up in my mouth a little. But that certainly would explain all the secrecy around whatever she was doing on her laptop.

"I've made an online dating profile for you on eligible.com."

Oh no!

"You've been getting a few responses."

Oh no! Oh no!

"I've chatted with a couple of them and they're really nice girls dear."

Triple oh no! SHE wasn't online dating … I was!

"Mom," I groan in exasperation, as I sit down on the sofa beside her and open her laptop back up, turning it so I can read the screen.

It's open to my personal profile on eligible.com

My dating site name is … Steven. I clench my teeth. My mom, bless her naïve soul, has used my real name. I don't see my last name on it, however, and say a silent prayer in thanks for small mercies.

I'm 49. 49!

And I've grown from my usual 5'10" to 6'1''.

I silently wondered how I'd pull that illusion off, hoping I'd never have to.

I have my own home, no mention of living with my mom. I enjoy hunting, fishing, boating and hockey.

"Mom, I've never even seen a hockey game!" I exclaim in disbelief. Whatever happened to truth in advertising? I guess it didn't apply to dating sites.

"And what's this, I'm looking for mature, independent women?"

"It will keep the gold-diggers away, dear."

Great, I think, if I'm looking to date somebody's grandma, someone like …

Oh no!

Oh no, oh no, oh no. I see what she's done. She's set up a dating profile for me to attract people like … people like herself. She's literally choosing her own replacement. The irony is that, like moms everywhere, she thinks, deep down, that no one will ever really be good enough for me, her son. She doesn't need to worry, it's not like moms are replaceable, really. I can't imagine not having my mom as my mom.

The plain truth is, I'm not looking to date at all. I think about Anna and her blatant flirting. She's been batting her false eyelashes and leaning over my desk for nearly a year now. For my part, I have zero interest in becoming another rung on her career ladder. No thank you.

Besides, she's such a phony. Everything about her is phony. Except maybe her blind ambition. Even her accent is phony, I know – it came and went with the weather. I have to admit, though, she does look and sound great on video. Her viewer metrics are superb.

"Can you make a profile that will keep them all away?" I half-joke, turning the screen back to her. The old gal feels guilty, I know. She thinks I'm trapped here with her, that she's holding me back. From what, I don't know. I'm perfectly happy right where I am.

Oh, well. Let her have her fun, what harm could it do?

I find out two days later when I come home to find my mom and another lady about her age, engaged in pleasant conversation over tea and scones. Silvery hair, pleasantly plump, bi-focal glasses, she could be my mom's, or Mrs. Santa's, twin. Which might be nice to come home to after a 24-hour trip around the globe delivering toys, but was not necessarily every 21-year-old's dream. Certainly not mine.

"Oh Steven, there you are dear. This is Marjorie Robinson."

"Hello, Mrs. Robinson."

"Call me Marj," she coos, uncrossing and re-crossing her admittedly shapely legs. I'd seen The Graduate, and I didn't like where this was going.

"I was just explaining to Marjorie that you're really 29, that we put 49 to keep the silly young girls away. You know, because you're so mature for your age."

"You're quite the smooth talker, for 29," Marj purrs, "got a real way with words. And such smooth skin too."

This is getting creepy.

And what way with words? We just met. I'd never spoken with her in my life. What was going on here? Smooth talker? Me?

And then it clicked. My eureka moment. It all made sense. My mom had met Marj online! Pretending to be me. I can only imagine what she's been saying, but I'd rather not.

Yup, that's why she's been closing her laptop whenever I'm around

I've heard of May – December romances, and I don't really care one way or another what people do in their personal life – but in my own life, I'd at least like to try one May-May romance first. If I absolutely must. To keep my mom happy, if nothing else.

After what seems like hours, but was really only a few minutes, I excuse myself to edit some imaginary articles for tomorrow's paper.

"Urgent stuff. Can't wait. Nice to meet you. Have a nice night."

I wait until she's gone and then go back out to the living room.

"Well ...?"

"No, Mom."

"Not even ..."

"No, Mom. You should have saved yourself the trouble. I'm not interested. Since you're such a smooth talker with the ladies I know you'll find a way to let her down easy. And seriously … 49? And whose photo is that?"

And that's the end of that, I think. Mistakenly, as it turns out.

***

Exactly one week later, to the day, it happens again. Sort of. My mom put up a new profile in hopes of reaching a younger target audience, to put it in advertising terminology.

And, in that particular regard, it was certainly successful.

Pop!

I walk in the front door to the sound of bubble bum popping. My mom sometimes chews gum for fresh breath – thank God, she drinks so much coffee in a day – but she doesn't blow bubbles.

I round the corner of the foyer and my suspicions are confirmed.

Perched eagerly, if one can perch eagerly, on the edge of the sofa is a girl. Not a woman, a girl. There's a big difference. It was like one of those monster truck shows where the announcer yells: "We'll sell you the whole seat but you'll only need the edge".

"Hi," she giggles. "I'm Crystal. Crystal Waters." Another giggle.

Apparently she finds her name very amusing. Cute. And maybe all of 18. For a moment I seriously consider asking for ID.

"So, like, your, like, mom, like, let me in."

Pop!

"She, like, had to, like, do something?"

Her voice went up at the end. Like she was asking a question. If she says axe instead of ask, it's over. What am I thinking? It's over already. It hadn't ever begun. Period.

In my mind's eye, I push a button springing a hidden trap door beneath her seat, sending her plummeting into a pit of hungry alligators.

Too harsh? Okay, how about a pit of multi-colored marshmallows?

I don't care. Just. Get. Her. Out. Of. Here Now!

I haven't spoken yet.

"Hey," I say, stalling for time while I think of something to say. What would my mom, the smooth talker, say?

"Wow," I raise my eyebrows and look at my blank iPhone screen. "I just got a text. There's a one-hour sale on at If the Shoe Fits. If you leave now you can probably make it."

"Dude, like, ya-aaa," again with the odd vocal cadence. I didn't much care for it.

"But, like, dude, I, like, don't have a ride. Your mom, like, came and, like, you know, picked me up."

Oh yes, I know. I know.

"Can you, like, give me a ride, dude?" twirling her hair around her index finger.

"I can do better than that," I say. "I'll get you an Uber." That's it, I think. This is the last straw. I have to do something, anything, to make. It. Stop.

Unfortunately, it seems nothing short of bringing a girl home is going to satisfy my mom. And I don't see that happening any time soon.

Maybe she's right. Maybe I should get out more. Meet new people. But she's going about it all wrong, in my opinion. I prefer things to be more organic, more natural. When it happens it happens. And I certainly don't want to rush into anything. Nope, baby steps is the way to go – crawl before you walk, walk before you run. And never run with scissors. if I run at all.

***

I've seen the posters around the office for the annual company slow pitch tournament. I've never gone to watch, and certainly nobody has ever asked me to play. Just as well, I've never thrown or caught a ball – of any kind – in my life. The paper's social committee puts the tournament on every year as a way of bringing people from the different departments together. Good luck with that.

In reality, however, each department usually enters their own team and plays harder than they should for bragging rights and a $5 plastic trophy.

Hmm. Why not? Baby steps. And it will make my mom happy.

I pick up the pen laying on the sign-up sheet and put my name after the last name on the list, Tessa Toews. Tessa. Hmm.

Okay, done.

Now I need to bring a girl home AND learn to catch, although not necessarily in that order.

Still, I wish me luck.

Chapter 9 — Tessa

It's gone!

The folder's there, but it's as empty as Mother Hubbard's cupboards.

No sign of my interview video file. No notes. No contact info, although I suppose I could track that down easy enough. I did have the name and department at the Clinic.

It was all right here on my desktop in a folder labeled Enterprise.

Maybe I misplaced it. Saved it to a different folder by mistake. I'll do a search.

Nothing. Maybe it's in the trash, somehow. Nope.

It's gone. Gone, gone, and gone!

Why, oh why did I not back that up to flash drive?!

This could mean my career and I was too what, lazy? Careless? To back it up.

My heart is beating like crazy. Too fast, too fast. I'm having trouble breathing.

This must be what a panic attack is like. Not good, not now, not here. Breathe, Tessa, slow and deep.

My dad and I occasionally do yoga along to online sessions and I close my eyes and slip into a deep breathing rhythm. In through the nose, chest rises. Out through the mouth, chest falls.

When I open my eyes I notice a crowd has gathered around the TV monitor in the center of the newsroom. We're usually tuned in to a couple of things, CNN, Al Jazeera, Turner News, among others.

Wiping a solitary tear from my cheek — thank goodness everyone's watching the TV and didn't see my cry — I get up and go over to see what all the fuss is about.

It's Anna. Of course.

She's doing a live broadcast for the morning news show, we call it that even though it was online only, and I recognize the buildings of the Mayo Clinic in the background. Anna is talking into a microphone. Somebody turns up the volume.

"Researchers here at the Mayo Clinic in Rochester, in an exclusive interview with this reporter, announced today they've made a major breakthrough in their research into the treatment of Multiple Sclerosis, a neurodegenerative disease affecting an estimated one million Americans. Per capita," she went on, playing up her phony southern accent to the max, "our state has the highest number of MS cases in the country."

My research. My story.

I don't remember much after that. It's kind of blurry.

Anna is still talking, but I don't really hear her.

Then Dr. Farquason appears on screen. I recognize her office, her face, her voice. Her answers.

Because it's my interview. THAT's my interview!

That fish-lipped, large-mouthed bass Anna has stolen my story. Hook, line and sinker!

Those are MY video clips. That is MY interview. She's dubbed the interview video in between her live shots to make it look like she's done the interview. I've been cut out of all the shots, my voice too. It's as if I didn't exist. And, to people like Anna, I don't.

To a narcissist like Anna, the whole world, everyone and everything in it, exists solely for her personal gratification. The world is her oyster.

I don't need the world to be my oyster. Not the whole world, anyways. But stumbling across the odd clam now and again might be nice.

Its bad enough I have to compete with her tall, willowy, blonde and buxom phony southern girl charms, but this?

How do I compete with this?

With outright theft?

In baseball, I'd turn up the heat. I'd up my effort level. I would simply out-try everyone else.

But it was one thing when it meant running faster, hitting further or sliding harder ... it was something totally different to sabotage coworkers in your office. Wasn't it?

And it WAS sabotage. It was intellectual theft. It was just plain ... not fair.

Hmmph. Fair.

When I was little and would complain about something not being fair my dad would always say the same thing: "Who ever told you life was going to be fair, Tessa. Get used to it."

He was right, of course, but as a ten-year-old who's just been called out at home plate when you were clearly safe ... it was a little too ... honest.

Nope, life isn't fair, that's for sure.

Otherwise, how do people like Anna Nordstrom, if that's even her real name, get what they want and people like me – nice people – don't?

And what could I do about it anyways? I'm just an intern. She has a year of experience.

Among other, more tangible, assets.

Probably around the same time my dad told we life wasn't fair, he also suggested it wasn't a good thing to be a tattletale. A squealer. A snitch. A narc.

In his books, it was nearly as bad to be a tattletale as to be the one being told on. Depending on the offence, of course. We're talking petty kid stuff here, not capital murder cases. In this instance, however I feel I have no choice.

I know Steve will have seen the broadcast in his office. He keeps one of his desktop monitors split into four screens so that it's logged into several different news sources all day, every day.

I pull myself together, nobody's noticed me at the back of the crowd, turn on a dime and March self-assuredly to Steve's office, determined to maintain my professionalism. Especially in front of super stuffy Steve. Or S-cubed, as Suzi had abbreviated it when I'd once used that rather unflattering characterization in front of her.

So far, so good.

One foot in front of the other. Deep breaths. No tears. Tears at work are not cool.

I will not cry. I will not cry. I will not cry.

And I'm not, as I knock on Steve's door.

"Come in," he says, glancing up. "Tessa."

Steve's door is always open. I close it and sit down.

"Anna stole my story!" I blubber, the tears flowing fast and free.

Chapter 10 — Steve

"Anna stole my story!"

Oh great, here come the waterworks. Seems to be a thing with interns. Of all gender identities.

I grab a Kleenex from the box on my desk and hand her one. I can't even understand what she's saying, she's crying so hard, the words coming in fragments.

"Whoa, slow down, Tessa. What story?"

"That's … my … story," she blubbers, pointing at my computer, where Anna Nordstrom is just finishing up another live morning show feed.

A really good one. Better than I'm used to seeing from her. Great news. Great source. Obviously good interview questions to elicit the responses I'd heard.

It was probably some of Anna's best work.

"That's my news cast," Tessa says, clear enough now for me to understand her now. "THAT'S my enterpriser!"

I look from my monitor, where Anna is just signing off — "This is Anna Nordstrom reporting live from the Mayo Clinic."

Tessa looks like she might be sick.

She's still trembling, but she isn't crying any more. That's good.

I have no time or use for tears. Yet I feel – what? – Bad for her.

"That was my enterpriser assignment," she says again, slowly, nodding her head at the screen. "I had a few video clips for the website and audio of the full interview that I was going to write-up for print. It was all on my computer. Now it's not. I did the interview two days ago. I got the idea from my mom. She works there. The Mayo Clinic. Where Dr.

Farquason works. But not in the same department. She's edited me out of the video and put the clips in around her own live shots.

"I hadn't told you about it yet because I wanted, well, I didn't want you to give it to someone else, like Anna. It's a good story."

It was a great story.

If it was Tessa's, and Anna had stolen it that was a big deal. And not just to Tessa.

No, it was a huge deal. Punishable by immediate termination.

I suppress a chuckle. Laughing likely wouldn't go over well in this situation. Even I know that.

Well, dismissal from the paper anyways. Not, literally, termination.

"These are serious accusations, Tessa. Do you have any proof? Anything on your computer? Did you print anything out or back anything up?"

The look on her face gives me her answers.

I frown. I back up everything I write on a flash stick daily. Emails, everything.

I know people make fun of me because I have a list of my lists, and where each is located, but I can locate items easily and I never lose anything. Ever.

If the computers at the office went down, I could carry on from home, or wherever.

Now, here this girl was in front of me because she hadn't done the simplest of things, back up her work.

No, that's not fair, not if her work WAS stolen. That's NOT her fault.

And I didn't rule the possibility out. Especially where Anna Nordstrom was concerned. That girl had claws.

"You can call Dr. Farquason. She'll tell you I interviewed her."

"I'm sorry, Tessa. I can't do that."

"Why not?" she says. "I can get the number again," her voice pleading.

"We can't do that, Tessa. For starters, think about how it makes the newspaper look. How it would affect our reputation. If word got out we had reporters stealing each other's assignments – without management having a clue – well, it makes us look bad. All of us."

Especially me and Mr. Osborne.

"Second, it's not really fair to drag Dr. Farquason into our internal issues. These kind of family matters are best kept in-house."

"But ..." she starts, before I silence her with a wave of my hand.

"Hear me out. Third, and this is what YOU should be concerned about Tessa, is – even if you had proof that Anna stole your story – which you don't – YOU still need a story.

"The rules of the internship are pretty rigid. We don't make them, it's a corporate thing. Its three months. At the end of it, if you want a positive referral or even a job, you have to have completed an enterpriser.

"The worst part is, you've lost a little over a month of the allotted time to work on it. You'll have to come up with another idea, Tessa. I'd suggest you do it quickly."

She nodded.

"Oh, and Tessa, get my approval first this time."

"Uh huh."

"And back up your work."

I genuinely feel bad for her. She's a good kid. And Anna's a, well, I try not to use that kind of language.

But I have my own problems. My own fish to fry, as they say.

Whoever 'they' are. Certainly I've never caught, killed, gutted or fried a fish. Yuk.

I have to learn to catch by the company baseball tournament at the end of the month. And maybe throw too.

***

I went out to Walmart and bought myself a glove, for my right hand, because I'm right-handed, a baseball and one of those rebounder things that I can throw the ball against and have it bounce back to me so I can catch it.

Perfect! Who needs a dad when you have Walmart? I'll learn to throw AND catch at the same time!

We have a good-size backyard, with six-foot high fences, and I find myself – somewhat surprisingly – looking forward to developing my skills in the privacy of my own backyard and then stepping out onto the field at the company tournament and amazing everyone with my athletic prowess.

At least that's the plan.

But first, a chat with Mr. Google, just to see how things are done. Mr. Google has taught me how to change spark plugs in the lawn mower and tie a bowtie, I'm sure he knows how to perform a simplistic primitive ritual like catch a ball.

I'd even learned how to swim by watching video demonstrations and had made it to the Lifeguard level. Of course, I'd never had to put those lessons to the test in actual water. And I hoped I'd never have to.

As it turns out, Mr. Google had many, many examples of how to throw, catch, hit, slide, chew tobacco and rearrange one's crotch. Lots of videos of people getting hit in the genitals by baseballs and other people laughing at them as they rolled on the ground, curled into the fetal position in what appeared to be hilarious pain.

Baby steps. One thing at a time. First, I just need to learn how to catch. I'll worry about the throwing thing later.

Nearly every video shows two people playing catch. Starting close and gradually moving further apart. Looks easy. I'll try that with my rebound thing.

In some of the beginner videos, they show a kid just tossing the ball straight up in the air and catching it over and over. That seems like a good place for me to start.

I toss the ball up and … it lands over the fence in the neighbor's yard.

I go get it and try again. Straight up this time. Better. Boy that ball sure looks small up there, getting bigger, bigger, as it falls back down – ouch!

I put up my glove to catch the ball, in doing so accidently blocking my view of said ball, which teaches me a quick lesson by bonking me on the top of the head. I can't help chuckling because I'd seen some blooper videos of major league baseball players doing the exact same thing. Well, maybe not exactly. The balls they missed were dropping down from just under 200 feet up in the air. I was tossing mine up about ten or twelve.

Okay, I'm kind of getting the hang of it. Tossing it up anyways. I keep closing my glove too soon though, the ball glancing off the outside and onto the ground. Except for the couple of times it hits my face.

I ditch the John Lennon glasses and retrieve an old pair of plastic-rimmed, Band-Aid-repaired ones from my top dresser drawer where I file all my old pairs of glasses.

Hmm. These glasses don't seem to help me catch any better. It's probably just the height thing. You know, looking straight up like that. Giving me vertigo.

I decide to try my 'bouncy thing' now. Maybe I'll be better at catching the ball if it's coming at me on a level trajectory. I'll just throw the ball at the target, hold out my glove, and let the ball bounce back into it. Easy peasy.

My first throw misses the target completely. In fact, it misses the entire rebounder, rolling under the fence into the neighbor's yard. Again.

I try again. With the same result. And again. And again. Throw. Retrieve. Repeat.

It reminds me of the instructions on a shampoo bottle. Einstein's definition of insanity pops into my head: 'doing the same thing over and over again and expecting different results'.

On the other hand, practice makes perfect and certainly I've got the time to practice. If there's one thing I have plenty of in the evenings, it's time.

There. That one hit the net. Not the target, but the net.

Uh oh, here it comes back at me. Ouch!

Right in the shin bone. That ball's hard!

I've got to hit higher up on the netting. The target would be nice.

I throw again. It's higher, but goes off to one side of the netting and bounces back to the side without my glove.

What now?

The ball goes flying past my left side about waist high, hitting the wall of our house a mere couple of inches from our kitchen's rear bay window.

That was close, too close, for comfort. I don't feel like having to call for an emergency bay window replacement tonight.

So I turn my target slightly, check to see what's behind me and throw another one.

Oh. That felt not too bad. That's probably my best throw yet.

It's coming back … Right. At. Me.

It hits me in the man parts.

I'm on the ground, and not laughing.

"Stevie," I hear my mom call from the back door. "Are you okay? It looked like that ball hit you right in the Oscar Meyer."

No, I'm not. And yes, it did.

That's what we'd called 'it', my privates, for as long as I could remember. Oscar Meyer.

The song from the old ad campaign flashes through my brain.

"My wiener has a first name, it's O-s-c-a-r."

I didn't really care for the name right now.

"Tell mommy where it hurts, dear."

I didn't much care to do that either.

At the moment, however, I'm in no position to argue.

***

I shift the ice pack resting lightly between my legs.

Now I know where the term 'numb nuts' came from.

Joking aside, I still haven't solved my problem. I still need to learn to catch. And throw.

Most of the videos show people throwing the ball back and forth. Kids, adults, kids with adults. Fathers with sons.

Who could I throw a ball with?

Not Mom. Not Mr. Osborne.

And that was it. That was my entire list of friends.

 If I had a Facebook page, I'd have the record for the fewest friends ever. Two. Wait, no, one. Mr. Osborne doesn't Facebook. His wife does, but he doesn't. Maybe she'd be my friend, so maybe two.

In any case, I didn't know anyone who I could play catch with?

Or did I?

What about Tessa Toews?

Her name was right above mine on the baseball tournament sign-up list.

I also know from her resume that she played high school ball.

Some people included that kind of thing, thinking it showed they were a 'team' player.

Personally, I've never thought it was relevant to being a journalist.

Based on Anna's behavior, I wonder if I should take that more into account in future.

Anna … I shake my head … what if she DID steal that story?

And it came to me.

Maybe the ice bag on the old Oscar Meyer was giving me the inspiration I needed!

Something was.

I'll help Tessa find another enterpriser. A good one. And she can help me learn to catch.

I'll talk to her about it at work tomorrow morning.

Chapter 11 — Tessa

Steve wants to see me in his office.

Maybe about the story thing, I don't know.

He's right that there's not much that can be done.

It's not like there are video security cameras in the newsroom or anything.

I mean, who'd want to steal the news?

It's not like we have cash on hand or anything.

And our computers, other than in the graphics department, aren't exactly state-of-the-art.

Probably about the story, but what about it?

"Good morning, Tessa," he says, smiling.

Yes, that's definitely a smile.

And a nice one. Nice teeth. Dimples.

Why have I not noticed before?

And why am I noticing now?

"Hi Steve. What's up?"

I've learned to be direct with this guy. Cut straight to the chase. He likes that.

"Straight to the point. I like that. Let me get straight to the point too. I have a proposal for you. I can help you with your enterpriser, but I have something I need you to help me with in return. It would involve some after-hours work on your part."

Is this guy saying what it sounds like he's saying?

What's this 'something' he needs help with?

It better not be what I think it is.

It's always the quiet, prim and proper ones that end up being the serial killers, just like on TV.

"He lived with his mom and kept to himself," the neighbors always said after the killer is caught.

Steve, who lives with his mom and keeps to himself ... what do I really know about him?

Away from work, nothing. For all I know, he lives on a pig farm in the foothills and feeds his victims to the hogs. Okay, maybe I'm being a little too dramatic.

Could be just a simple slave pit in the basement, like in Silence of the Lambs.

I hope not, because aside from being too short to climb out, I bite my nails (so they don't break playing baseball is my excuse, if anyone asks) and wouldn't be able to get much grip on the stone walls.

"Um," I hear a voice that sounds just like mine say.

I needed that enterpriser, but ...

Chill out, Tessa, and hear what he has to say. Chances are he's not a mass murderer. Probably.

It reminds me briefly of the old joke: A man picks up a hitchhiker and the hitchhiker asks him, "Aren't you afraid I might be a serial killer or something?"

"Naa," says the driver, "what are the chances of having two serial killers in the same car?"

Okay, he's probably NOT a serial killer. But he wants ... something, something that's "after hours".

"Sure," I hear the voice that sounds like mine say. "What have you got in mind?"

Did I really just say that? Agree to meet this guy away from work? Am I having some kind of disembodied experience right now?

Nope, this is really happening. To me.

If this geek hits on me, I'm punching him right in the face. Job or no job.

"Excellent," he says, clapping his hands together, startling me back into my earthly body.

He's certainly excited about … whatever.

"I have an idea for your enterpriser," he says. "The idea itself isn't that unique, not really 'stop the presses!' kind of stuff, but – if you take my advice and do things the way I suggest – I think you'll be able to deliver a great enterpriser. I'm thinking big here, Tessa. A two-page spread in City. Maybe 5,000 words for print and I'm thinking some nice video for online. It's ambitious, but I think we can do it, Tessa."

We.

"We can do it," he said.

So he's going to help me. With the idea, the angle, the contacts, hopefully the story and video editing too. It seems like an unfair advantage, but then Anna's stealing of my story wasn't exactly fair either.

All's fair in love and journalism, I guess.

"That's awesome!" definitely my voice now, for sure. "I, we, can do it. Thanks. I promise to back it up this time."

"I know you will, Tessa."

There's that smile again. Like a ray of sun peeking out from behind the clouds.

And now the moment of truth. The moment of no return.

The single most important moment of my career so far.

Time to find out what the nerdy guy behind the bowtie and John Lennon glasses wants in return.

I hope it's not what men usually want. Please, no.

The thought of my career, my entire future, hinging on what Steve, my boss, needs help with is nauseating. If he hits on me now, I might puke first, and then punch him in the face after.

"So, what do YOU need help with?" I ask.

"Well," he starts, "it's a little out of the ordinary."

Oh great. What sort of weirdness is this guy into?

"I see you signed up for the baseball tournament. I signed up too … and I don't know how to catch. Will you teach me how to catch, Tessa? I know you know how to play. We'd have to practice in the evenings, so no one could see us together. I've got a big back yard. If you're not comfortable, we could do it at your place. Play catch."

Play catch?!

That's his big request? He wants someone to play catch with?

THAT I could do!

I breathe a huge sigh of relief, laugh, and it finally dawns on him what he's said.

"Oh. No. No. No, Tessa. I'm sorry. I didn't realize how that sounded. I don't think that way. I …"

He's cute when he's embarrassed, when he blushes. In a nerdy sort of way.

"No worries," I cut him off.

I'm getting the better part of this deal, by far!

I mean, how hard could it be to teach a grown man to catch? How bad could this guy be?

"Have you ever played?"

"Just with myself."

"Baseball, I mean."

I'm teasing him. Now who's putting their foot in their mouth?

"That's what I meant."

He's blushing again. Funny. I might be enjoying this a little too much.

"What about as a kid with your friends? Or your dad?"

"I didn't have friends and … I don't have a dad."

Oh.

I don't know what to say to that. It's just so ... sad.

"Sure, I'll teach you."

How could I say no?

"We've only got a couple of weeks 'til the tourney, though, so we'll have to do some evenings, maybe weekends. If you're serious, that is."

"As serious as you are about your enterpriser."

Hmm. I doubt that. But we'll see.

"I'm serious about nobody knowing though. Other than my mom and your family. You can't tell anyone."

I replay the discussion in my head over and over all day long. And each time it ends the same – I'm teaching my boss how to throw and catch a baseball in return for him helping me on the most important assignment – so far – of my fledgling career.

It's his job to guide me and edit my work, but he was going above and beyond what he'd ever done for any other intern. Or so says Suzi.

"I think he likes you," she says when I tell her of the arrangement.

It's been approximately three hours since I promised Steve I wouldn't tell anyone. So much for secrets.

"Ha, right," I laugh in response.

"Or," she pauses for effect, "or, maybe YOU like HIM."

"Like's a pretty strong word. More like ... pity."

Was that what it was? Maybe not pity, but I did feel bad for him.

"It's strictly a business arrangement. He helps me, I help him. That's it. Seriously."

"Sure," says Suzi. "Whatever you say."

It's obvious she has her doubts. About my intentions, or his, I don't know.

But I AM serious.

Steve's my boss. I have no interest in him 'that way' whatsoever.

It's not like I felt a spark or anything.

And, based on what I now know about Steve, I'm not sure he'd know a spark if it hit him with 1,000 volts.

I mean, the guy can't even catch!

Nope, that's one thing I won't have to worry about. No danger there.

I can't see myself ever falling for a non-athlete, especially one who lives with his mom and dresses like Mr. Rogers.

No, Steve Sondergaard doesn't check any of my boyfriend boxes.

Not that I really have a checklist.

Some people do, I know.

When I was in grade ten, for my sweet 16 birthday, my mom and dad both gave me their boyfriend checklists. Just in case.

The irony was, if they'd taken the time to compare lists, they'd have seen what I had – they didn't check too many of each other's boxes.

I didn't keep the lists, but I remembered some of the items on them.

They didn't put their names on them, but I could tell whose was whose.

My dad's list included items like:

• Has a job
• Has a strong work ethic
• Is nice to Tessa
• Not an alcoholic or drug addict
• Laughs at my dad jokes

All good, common sense, qualities you'd want in a potential mate.

My mom's list was a little more detailed and included education level, occupation, income, age, height and weight restrictions as well as supplying a full genetic profile.

My best guess is that if I ever want to get married, she'll want a full genealogy and family medical history from the lucky fella.

Has his own home was right up there on her list.

I knew exactly what she'd say when I told her about our arrangement, and the fact Steve lived with his mom.

***

"Classic Oedipus complex," she analyzed over a scrambled eggs and hash browns dinner.

My dad had started trying to "mix things up a bit", as he put it, with dinner, and was on an egg kick.

Tonight was scrambled. The perfect dinner for my mixed-up life.

Last night had been fried eggs sunny side up with sticks of bacon arranged to look like a smiling face. I wish.

"He wants to kill his father and marry his mother," she drones on.

"He doesn't have a father."

She looks up at me, eyebrows raised in a silent question.

"No, he didn't kill him."

At least, I didn't think so. I never thought to ask.

I suppose I couldn't rule out the possibility … maybe I should do a Google search?

And what, see if he's been arrested for suspicion of murder?

My mom is still talking.

Something about somebody hanging themselves, pleasant family dinner table banter which is starting to sound to me a lot like the teachers on the old Charlie Brown specials: "Waa, waa waa waa waa."

Mom's point of view was a little extreme, bordering on clinically insane.

Besides, there was nothing there between Steve and I. There wasn't anything to talk about.

The smart thing here was to not engage.

"Great eggs, Dad, just the way I like them!"

Chapter 12 – Steve

That went well.

I'll help Tessa with her enterpriser and she'll help me learn to catch.

We have two weeks until the ball tournament and a little more than a month until Tessa's internship is up and her big story due.

Everything is falling into place nicely. Just the way I like it.

It's … perfect. What could possibly go wrong?

We weren't 'dating', so I wasn't really breaking any rules – written or otherwise – or risking my job by dating an underling. Underling. I guess that's what she is. Technically. I don't really think of her that way. She's just another intern. Who happens to be a girl? That's all. No biggie.

So why are my palms sweating?

Not that I'd have the nerve to ask her out anyways. Who am I kidding, I've never asked anyone out. What kind of future could I offer her, or any girl, for that matter, living with my mom?

And didn't she get those flowers from her boyfriend the other week?

Besides … why am I even thinking this?

She's teaching me to catch. That's it.

And I'm helping her with her assignment.

Period. End of story.

Nope, there was nothing personal involved. Not from my end. This was strictly business.

Tessa wasn't the girl for me. Probably

Chapter 13 — Tessa

"Sit down, Tessa."

Uh oh. Steve's voice is different. He's always a kind of bland monotone, but there's something else there today. Hurt? He seems upset.

We're supposed to start playing catch tonight and working on my new enterprise story tomorrow. I wonder if it's something to do with that.

"Tessa, I just got out of Mr. Osborne's office."

This wasn't about playing catch.

He put a copy of today's paper on his desk, open to page 7 of the City section.

It was an advertising feature, an advertorial for a new 'miracle' product, Bob's Wood Stain. The article at the top of the page was circled in red and, near the end of the article, circled in red was the word 'feces'.

"Osborne just tore me a new one for this. Which seems appropriate given the nature of the error. What happened, Tessa?"

I know immediately. This is not good. Not good at all.

The sentence was supposed to read: Bob's Wood Stain is perfect for preserving wooden decks, siding and fences.

Except there was no 'N' in fences. Making it feces. Which I doubt anyone wants to preserve. Unless it's from Elvis, or a dinosaur or something.

Even then. Not. Good.

"Tessa?"

"I ... I used spell check," I say, knowing that's not what he wants to hear. It's the truth. But it's not what he wants to hear.

His disappointment is written all over his face. As obvious as a child's crayon drawing on the living room wall. He's tense. He's mad. But mostly disappointed. I can feel it, almost smell it.

"Oh, well, it's all good then," he says sarcastically. "It's spell check's fault."

I was supposed to show it to the client for approval before submitting the text for a layout. Why hadn't I done it? it's just an ad feature, I'd thought at the time, for a stupid wood stain, so why do a full proof read? And hadn't they already proofed it with the writer? It's just an ad feature.

"You DO know what feces IS, don't you?"

"Yes," I say. Still looking down at the story, not wanting to meet his eyes. Not wanting him to see the tears in mine. Again.

I'd let him down. And got him in trouble. And all while he was trying to help me.

So far. Maybe that was about to change.

"Monkeys throw it. Some reporters write it. Don't be one of them!"

"I'm sorry, Steve, I …"

"I know. You used spell check. You thought it was good enough. But it's not, Tessa. I don't know if you were being lazy or careless, or both, but it's not 'good enough'. I expect better from you. Consider this a learning experience and don't let it happen again."

And there it was. He expects better from me.

He isn't firing me. He thinks I have potential.

I hope he's keeping me for my potential as a journalist, and not just to play catch with.

I made a mistake. I owned it. It was okay to make mistakes, my dad once told me, and it just means you're trying. It's when you keep repeating the same mistakes, he said, that you have a real problem. He'd also told me that – if you paid attention – you could learn from other people's mistakes without having to make them all yourself.

I decided then and there that was the way to go, in baseball and life in general. I wasn't perfect, and didn't claim to be … but I owned my mistakes and tried not to repeat them.

"I know you think it's 'just an ad feature'," says Steve, "but what do you think pays the bills around here? Keeps the lights on? The presses turning? Pays our salaries?"

I didn't know anything about the business side of newspapers. They totally ignored that at J school.

"Not our dwindling print readership," he says, "with a shrinking subscriber base. Without advertising, we're out of business."

I don't say anything. I'm just listening. This was all news to me. Why hadn't our Profs taught us this stuff? This was important.

"Tessa, that ad was worth $3,000. We have to run it again, for free. I have to try to find space for it in tomorrow's City section. Probably have to kill something else, a story, to fit it in last minute."

I had cost the company $3,000. About a month's pay, if I was being paid.

Maybe it was a good thing I was an intern, or they might dock my pay.

As it was, I was lucky to keep my job.

"You're lucky to keep your job."

***

On my way back to my desk, I overhear Mr. Osborne talking on his phone as he relays the story to someone.

"Feces," I hear him say, loudly. And then … laughing.

I'm not eavesdropping, I tell myself, hesitating ever so slightly in the hall outside his office. He just has a loud voice and I happen to be walking by.

And … he's … laughing. Yes, he's definitely laughing about it. From the sounds of it he was talking to someone named Bob. The ad client!

"Yes, he was sorry it happened. Yes, he'd spoken to the people responsible and could guarantee it wouldn't happen again."

You've got that right, Oz, old boy. So laugh it up now, at my expense. Why was I beating myself up about this when this guy, THE boss, obviously thought it was so funny?

I hear him thank Bob for having a sense of humor about it – so the client thinks it's funny too – and promise to run the entire full page, not just the article, again in tomorrow's paper.

For free… making my mistake, a single omitted 'N', worth $3,000.

Just like Steve said.

Chapter 14 - Tessa

"THAT'S what you're wearing?!"

It's after dinner and, as agreed upon, we're in Steve's backyard to play catch.

Or, as I prefer to call it, Baseball 101.

Because this dude needs to learn a lot more than just how to catch a ball.

I mean, seriously, who wears a sweater vest, blue polka-dot bowtie and dress shoes to play catch? Bowties are for ventriloquist puppets, not baseball players.

"Shhhh," he puts his finger to his lips. His luscious full lips. Now where did THAT come from? Just the writer in me coming out, I think.

"My mom's asleep. Try to keep your voice down please."

He's got a really nice house, only a few neighborhoods away, as it turns out, in an older part of town.

It's a farm-style two-story home, small but cute with white wood siding – no idea if he used Bob's Woodstain or not – and bright yellow shutters and trim around the windows and doors. An obviously homemade wood planter box overflows with blooming flowers in a multitude of colors.

I know where I'd come for my next fake boyfriend bouquet. Ugh. I still had THAT problem at work, and Anna wouldn't let it go.

The front yard is surrounded by a waist-high white picket fence, freshly painted, by the looks of it. We're around back, surrounded by a six-foot, fortress-like white-washed wood fence. Somebody's been doing a lot of painting around here. I wonder if he got a deal from Bob's Woodstain for running that ad feature again.

Na that was just this morning and this paint is at least, what, a week or two old?

"Okay, sorry."

Asleep?! It's only 7 p.m.!

Maybe she's a nurse or something and works shifts.

"Alright," I say more quietly. "Let's see you throw one at your rebounder and catch it."

OMG!

Or, as Suzi might have said in this situation, "KMN!"

Kill me now!

The glove he's pulled out is a plastic child's glove. It looks tiny on his hand. His right hand. I know from work Steve's right-handed – hmm, funny I'd noticed that – he moussed with his right hand, which meant he'd bought the wrong-handed glove. If you're right-handed, you catch with your left. You throw with your right.

He's got a ball in his hand, but it's a hardball, for fastball, not a slow pitch softball. And he's got it in his left hand. His form is … I can't think of any other word than spastic, as ball after ball bounces off the tall fences.

He throws like a … a person who doesn't know how to throw. I won't say girl, because I know some girls who can really chuck it. Myself included.

Of course, using the correct hand might make a difference. Maybe. Hopefully.

Based on what I've witnessed so far – whoa, here it comes off the metal frame of the rebounder and right back at me – it couldn't be any worse. No way.

I catch the ball and flip it, underhand, back to him.

"Okay Mighty Casey," I say, taking his glove from him, "let's go."

"Go where? I thought we were playing catch. And who's Mighty Casey?"

"Oh, we are going to play catch," I assure him. "But not tonight. And Google him. Come on."

I hold out my hand like he's a, what? A child? And he takes it as I lead him back to my car.

"Okay Freddy," I say, "let's go to Rick's."

"Who's Freddy?" asks Steve, looking around. "And who's Rick?"

This was going to be fun.

***

I've been to Rick's Sporting Goods lots of times, but Steve's eyeballs blink wide open like a cartoon characters as we walk in the doors.

Rick's is pretty impressive, I'll admit. I can spend hours here, just looking. Looking at all the great sporting goods and camping gear I can't afford. I can only imagine the assault on the senses it is for a guy like Steve.

I wonder if he's ever been to Disneyworld. If he's this excited to visit Rick's …

"Wow," says Steve as we make our way to the baseball area, passing through several other different sport sections along our journey.

"What's this?"

"A lacrosse stick."

"What's this?"

"A fishing float tube. It has legs built in."

"Neat."

"Ya. Here's the baseball stuff."

One wall is taken up by baseball shoes and another by a rack of bats. The adjacent shelves are lined with balls, batting gloves, ball caps, batting and catcher's helmets and other accessories. Completing the nook is an entire wall of gloves of varying sizes, styles and colors from several big-name manufacturers like Rawlings and Spalding. There are first baseman's gloves and catcher's mitts, and plenty of affordably-priced gloves that will be fine for Steve.

I'll have him try a few on, see what fits and which he can open and close easily. It's not like there's time for him to properly break it in.

Steve is the proverbial kid in a candy store as he tries on gloves and, eventually, some cleats.

"Okay," he announces.

It's now a quarter to 9. We've been here at Rick's well over an hour-and-a-half and the store's getting ready to close.

"These will do for me," he says, holding up a sleek-looking pair of Nike cleats and a bright blue glove.

"Go with the black," I say. "Or brown. Blue's for … I almost say it again. "Blue's not your color."

He puts the blue back and grabs the same model in black. Hmm, this guy actually takes my advice. A lot of guys won't, especially when it comes to sports. Interesting.

"Now," he says. "I need some proper pants, shirt, socks, hat and anything else you can think of. I think they're getting ready to close, we can grab the shoes and glove and come back earlier tomorrow night to get the rest."

"Tomorrow night," I look him in the eye, "I'll be teaching you how to catch. I'll talk to the manager, I'm sure they'll let us keep shopping."

That's just how I roll. The single-mindedness. The focus on the goal. That's who I am.

And stay open they did. They herd all the other customers out at 9 and let us keep shopping. And shopping, and shopping.

Steve asks the manager to bring a cart and tosses in the cleats and glove. Or, rather, places them in carefully. I would have tossed them.

He's also grabs a couple pairs of black sweat pants, a half dozen pairs of white athletic socks, a couple of ball caps, two-T-shirts and one sweat shirt. All Nike.

"I like to look coordinated," he says, when I ask why. "And that swoop thing is neat."

"Swoosh."

He's in front of the bat rack now. I thought this was about catching?

"What's a good bat, Tessa?"

"This one's good," I say, hefting a nice Easton aluminum model. It's worth close to $300.

"Great," he says, "put it in the cart."

"Let's get one of each," he says. "Grab the best wood bat and let's get one of those composite carbon fiber ones over there too."

That was at least $800 worth of bats.

"We might need them for the tournament," he says.

He puts a dozen regulation slow pitch balls in the cart, along with catcher's mask – I'd mentioned casually that they don't usually have them at these tournaments – a couple of batting helmets and a cheaper model extra glove – for both hands – "just in case someone forgets theirs."

Finally, with the manager anxiously looking at the clock as it's about to strike 10, we're done.

"One last thing," says Steve, spying the largest sports duffel bag in the store and tossing it on top of the cart. "We can take it all home in this."

"Sure," I say, a little bit taken aback.

I mean, this dude's just dropped close to a couple thou so he can learn to catch for a company baseball tournament.

"Um, isn't it kind of, um, a lot?"

"Money's not my problem, Tessa," he smiles.

There's that smile again.

"Learning to catch is. Do you want anything? New glove?"

"Uh, no ... thanks."

What am I supposed to say?

It's a nice gesture. But ... and this is a ME thing ... I don't like taking gifts from people.

Especially when they're my boss. Nope, he buying me things wasn't part of the deal.

Besides, my trusty old glove, Betsy, and I have been through a lot together. I can't let her go now, just because this ... this guy, wants to buy me a new one.

"I guess that's it, then," he says to the manager, flashing those pearly whites again.

"What did you say to get them to stay open," Steve asks as we load the goods into Freddy's back seat, the most action it's seen in forever. The trunk is already full of stuff, as usual.

"I simply told them I was Eddie Toews daughter," I grin and close the rear car door.

"No, really, what did you say?"

I start the car and the Rolling Stones' 'You Can't Always Get What You Want' is playing.

"Sometimes, Steve," I say, buckling my seatbelt and turning to face him.

Our faces are close. Too close. I need a bigger car.

"You just have to go for it and ask for what you want. You'd be surprised what people will do for you sometimes, if you just ask. If you don't ask, you never know. All they can do is say 'no'."

I use the rest of the drive to explain some of the rules of baseball, as best I can. There are A LOT of rules. And strategy. It is a lot to learn. But, then, Steve IS supposedly a genius, isn't he?

He seems pretty … normal … tonight.

"Okay, here we are," I say. "Steve Central. All ashore who're going ashore."

Do we shake hands? Fist bump? Salute? Hug?

"Thanks Tessa," he says, leaning in the door before he closes it, "for everything. This was fun."

"No worries," I say, putting my hand up for a high-five and wondering what "everything" means.

He puts his hand up against mine and, instead of high-fiving, laces his fingers in between mine in a strange kind of hybrid high-five handshake thing. Weird.

Chapter 15 — Steve

"I really enjoyed last night, thanks again," I say as Tessa sits down across from me.

She looks nice today. What's different? I can't quite put my finger on it.

"Me too," she says. "If this journalism thing doesn't work out I can always be a professional shopper."

She's funny. I like that. You have to be smart to be funny. And I like smart.

"Oh I wouldn't worry about that, Tessa. Not once you nail this enterpriser. You're going to have to do some interviews during the day, so I've arranged for Anna to pick up some of the ad feature stuff."

"I'll bet she's thrilled about that."

"I don't care. Call it payback, if it helps. The important thing is, you've got time to do these interviews and tell this story. It's all about telling the story, Tessa. Don't over-think it, and don't over-write it. Tell it like you'd tell your best friend sitting across the table having coffee. Be … conversational. I know you're good at that," I chuckle.

Professional shopper? This little spitfire could probably out-talk an auctioneer!

"It's not an entirely new idea. The topic's been covered before, many times, but not like we're going to do it. Everything prior's been in bits in pieces. Nothing as comprehensive as this."

She looks worried.

"Don't worry. I'll walk you through story angles, contacts, questions to ask and such. I'll suggest photo and video opps. We'll discuss structuring your story to complement our graphic design plans. It will be fun. Not as fun as shopping for a baseball glove, but fun," I smile, reassuringly, I hope. "We're going to do a huge piece on the homeless shelter, Home for Hope. Not a news piece, there's no breaking news or anything like that. And the story of the shelter – how it was founded, what it's purpose is, how many people it serves – has been done before. We want that info, we want the stats, but we'll put them in a color info graphic format, not text.

"What we're going to do is tell the stories BEHIND the story. We're literally going to tell people's stories. Who are they? Why do they do what they do? What makes them happy?" She's not saying anything. Okay, listening is good for now. "You might want to take notes," I say, as I launch into what I like to call Features 101.

"People love to read about other people, Tessa. That's why we try to run as many photos of people as we can in the paper. Just to put a face to a story. Because people need us to humanize it for them. To bring it home. To keep it real.

"The next time you stand in front of a magazine rack, count the ones that have a photo of a person on the cover. That's to help draw your eye to it and help it sell. The difference with what we're going to do is, we won't just be using stock photos or mug shots. I'm getting Dean Jeffries, our best photos and video guy, to go with you."

Dean had won international awards for photojournalism and was one of the few people who had been friendly to me when I started at the Star-Bulletin. He spent his days off as a course marshal at a local golf course and had a laid-back, easy-going way about him that helped put people at ease. He could take great photos of paupers as well as princes, and had.

"You're going to spend an entire day on site at the shelter. Maybe more. One of the workers there will take you through 'a day in the life of the shelter', explaining the day-to-day goings on. It's okay to mention other things that happen too. Other 'things'" – I emphasized the word – "they might deal with not on a daily basis, but as they occur.

"I've spoken to my contact there at length and she knows what we're looking for. She thinks it's a great idea too and has agreed to help you any way she can. She'll set you up with a couple of other people to interview too.

"I'll help you develop a question list, but consider it more of a coloring book than a road map. You don't have to stay on one direct path, as long as you stay inside the lines. We want to get into these people's heads, Tessa. We want to know everything about them. It's a long list of questions. Not all the answers will make it to your final draft, but the trick is to gather as much information as possible … so as to sift through it for what's truly important. It's finding those hidden nuggets of gold that bring the story to life for the reader."

She doesn't look as sure as I feel, so I go on.

"You're going to like this, Tessa. And I think you'll be good at it. There's a story behind every face, and it's not always what you'd think. You can't always judge a book by it's cover, as the saying goes. You'll see what I mean when you meet your contact.

"Here's her name and number," I say, passing her a post-it note.

Chapter 16 — Tessa

Back at my desk, I look at the number he gave me. Jenny 507-867-5309.

No time like the present, I think, punching in the number on my cell.

Ring number 1. Ring number 2.

"Home for Hope, Jenny here."

She sounds busy. Rushed.

"Hi Jenny. Tessa Toews here, from the Star-Bulletin. I got your number from Steve Sondergaard."

"Oh yes, Tessa! Hello. Stevie said you'd be calling. Good morning. How are you?"

Stevie?

"Great, thanks. Yourself?"

 I was beginning to see why some people like to cut through the small talk. For this assignment, however, it was important to develop a rapport with the interview subjects – all of them – and that meant using both my listening skills and my gift of the gab. The trick is to know when to use each.

"Busy," she sighs, "always busy. Unfortunately, peoples' need for food and shelter doesn't take any time off. Stevie told me all about your story idea and I think it's wonderful! Why don't you come by this Saturday and I'll give you the grand tour and introduce you to a couple of people you might want to talk to?"

MY story idea? Is that what Stevie, I mean Steve, told her?

"Saturday's great," I reply, trying hard to convey equal amounts enthusiasm and professionalism.

That gives me time to get my questions figured out and get Dean lined up for video and photos.

"What time?"

"Hmm. How about 10? That way we're done with breakfast and I've got time to show you around before lunch starts. That's when things really start hopping."

"How do you know Steve," I ask. "Does he volunteer at the shelter?"

There's no way he'd ever been a resident. Was there?

"No. I think he'd like to, but he doesn't have time, he's got his hands full already at home, you know, looking after his mom."

Looking after his mom? What was that all about? That's not quite the same as living with your mom. It's the same but somehow … different.

***

The Home for Hope is in an old brick building in a sketchy part of town. It's close to 10 a.m., and already there's activity out front of the center. One older fellow is loading what looks like all his worldly possessions into a grocery cart. Ready to travel … where?

Another fellow has a green garbage bag nearly bursting at the seams with empty bottles and cans, the results of a successful night of scavenging.

A few others, mostly men, but a couple of women, mill about aimlessly a few feet from the entrance.

I park Freddy around the corner and walk back toward the front door. Do I look down at the sidewalk? Do I look them in the eye? Will they ask me for money if I do? What's the procedure here? I'm pretty sure telling them I'm Ed Toews' daughter won't carry any weight with this crowd either. But his other advice was still good: smile and nod.

"HI," I smile and nod at the group nearest the door.

I'm glad I wore these old jeans and T-shirt. My regular office attire would have made me stand out.

"Good morning, ma'am," says the gent nearest the door.

Ma'am?

Maybe I stand out a little more than I thought, even in these old Levis.

"Allow me," he says, flashing a grin that's missing a couple of front teeth and holding the door open wide.

"Thanks," I say, smiling back. Trying hard not to flaunt my own perfect-in-comparison Chiclets.

You catch more flies with honey than vinegar. Especially male flies.

"Any idea where I can find Jenny?"

"Right here dear," I hear as she appears, as if out of nowhere, a bulging plastic bag of garbage in each hand. "I've just got to take these out to the bin."

I follow her out to the dumpster.

It's unrecognizable as a garbage bin, it's so covered in graffiti. Some of it pretty good.

"There's probably 50 layers of paint on that thing," she chuckles as we turn and head back in.

"Here we are," she says settling into an old and cracked leather chair behind an old wooden desk.

It's more like a closet than an office. There's Jenny's desk and chair, two folding metal chairs opposite, and a couple of small filing cabinets low enough to double as additional places to pile things.

One of the cabinets has a photo on it, I can see. A slim, auburn-haired woman – presumably Jenny – and a VERY handsome young man with dirty-blonde hair cut in a crew-cut.

He looks familiar.

"Oh, "she says, noticing me looking at the photo, "Stevie didn't tell you?"

Didn't tell me what?

"I'm Jenny Osborne. Sandy's wife."

Sandy? Who's Sandy?

"Sandford Osborne," she says, realizing it hasn't clicked for me yet.

"Mr. Osborne. The great and powerful Oz. Your boss."

Oh, THAT Sandy.

"Right," I say. Not exactly the wittiest comeback ever. "I thought he looked familiar. His hair's a lot whiter now."

That was a little better, but not much.

It never occurred to me that there might be a Mrs. Oz. Yet here she was, in the flesh … about to help me on my big assignment. I wonder if Oz knew.

"Yes, he knows people call him that," says Jenny. "Among other things, I'm sure. He doesn't care. He's got lots of friends here and we've had the same neighbors for close to 40 years. He's not at work to make friend. He's there to push people to do their best. To work just a little bit harder than they want to. To be the best that they can be. But you've probably noticed that."

Boy have I ever.

"It wasn't easy for Sandy," she says. "He was an orphan, you know. Abandoned, left in a cardboard box outside the entry to a center just like this. He was fostered out to an older couple, old enough to be his grandparents, but in those days you took what you could get. There weren't as many rules and screening procedures as there are today."

I just listen.

"The old Irishman carried a cane and wasn't shy to use it on both his wife and Sandy. Finally, one day, when the old man went to hit him, Sandy had had enough. He grabbed the cane, snapped it in half and walked out the door with just the clothes on his back."

"Wow."

I can't think of anything intelligent to say. So I listen.

"He lived on the streets for a year, in Boston, then got a fake ID and joined the army."

That explains the haircut.

"He got that haircut. And he also got an education. He worked in recruiting, writing copy for ads, posters and brochures encouraging young people to join the army, serve their country and see the world.

"When he transferred to communications, writing for the Armed Forces Weekly, the army agreed to pay for half his schooling if he signed on for another 4 years. Not coincidently the exact amount of time it would take to earn his journalism degree. So he did it. Not exactly your normal journalism career path."

"I had no idea," I say. Because I didn't.

"Nobody does. And let's keep it that way please. The less people know about him the better, is how he likes it. He doesn't want people to think he's soft."

"Soft?" I can't help but laugh out loud. "I don't think you have to worry about that."

"Sometimes," Jenny says softly, "the boys he wrote about didn't come back. The feature he wrote on them were some of the last words and photos the family had left to remember them by. Sandy always made a point of keeping track, of sending each family a framed copy of their son or daughter's article."

Hmm. Maybe writing obituaries and feature articles aren't quite as bogus as I thought.

"He sees a little of himself in Stevie. Someone with lots of potential, with both the brains and the work ethic to make it, if life hadn't conspired against him to hold him back. He's kind of like the son we never had. I mean we've had lots of foster kids over the years, some boys, but we always knew it was a temporary arrangement."

Foster kids? Mr. Osborne?

You certainly COULDN'T judge THAT book by its cover!

***

"But enough about our men, let's take that tour you've been waiting so patiently for."

OUR men?!

Exactly WHAT had Stevie, I mean Steve, told her?

"Our clientele aren't as stereotypical as people like to think," she says as we walk. "Many have mental health issues and either can't afford or can't figure out how to access treatment. We try to help with that. Many don't have family to turn to. In some cases, the families were abusing them while taking their welfare checks. We also deal with a lot of abuse issues – spousal, substance, child, sexual …"

There's another couple of small offices on the main floor, a room that used to be a small office but now functions as a small library, a 'quiet' room with three computers at desks and, at the end of the hall, a large lounge area with TV, foosball table, sofas, lounge chairs and coffee tables.

"These people don't even have anywhere to just sit down and be comfortable," she says.

"The two upstairs floors are dedicated to living spaces. They're small, but they're secure," she says. "This floor's just for men. The upstairs is for women. We can house 80 people, but it's not enough. It's never enough."

The rooms remind me of a college dorm room, only smaller since they're intended for single occupancy. A bed, a night table with two drawers, a lamp and a closet. The bare necessities. The community bathroom was at the end of the hall.

"The kitchen and dining hall are in the basement," she says, looking at her watch and pushing the door open. "We're just in time for lunch."

The room smells of hot food and … something else.

"Toes!" I hear my name bellowed from across the room, incorrectly.

I've heard that bellow before.

"Here for a free lunch?" says a grinning Mr. Osborne. "Back of the bus, young lady," he says, nodding towards the line-up of hungry street people.

THAT was the 'something else' I'm smelling.

"Hi, Mr. Osborne."

Well, he definitely knows his wife is helping me.

"Now Sandy," chides Jenny, "be nice. This isn't the office."

"That's right, Ozzy," sings out the man with the missing teeth. "This isn't the office."

He laughs and … Mr. Osborne laughs along with him.

Ozzy?!

I can't help but laugh too.

***

"Here's those other contacts. Doris has a cell phone. Her number's there. Micah doesn't. I'll set something up with him and let you know. I'm sure Stevie will let you out of the office. You're lucky to work for him. He's turned out to be a fine young man."

"Yes," I reply. "He has."

And kind. And honest. And loyal. And, if you could get past the bowties and sweater vests, not too hard to look at either.

Chapter 17 — Steve

So far, so good.

Tessa's been coming over every night for the past week.

I look at my cell phone to check the time.

"No watches on the ball field," she'd admonished me that first time.

She was on her way over right now, skipping dinner to come straight over after her meeting with Jenny.

I wonder how that went.

Tonight's our last chance to practice before there's an actual editorial team practice. We had a team meeting and voted on a name, proposed by Mickey in graphics, Creative Juices. He even designed a team logo of a hand squeezing the juice out of a baseball.

Hmm. Juiced baseballs. Where had I heard THAT before?

I gave him $500 out of my wallet and told him to get a dozen team jerseys made. Graphics people know how to get those kinds of things done quickly.

There she is.

"Hey, Tessa. How'd the meeting go?"

"Great … Stevie," she replies, smiling.

It's an infectious smile, and I smile back.

"She's got me set up with a couple of other interviews this week. I tried to do some research ahead of time, but neither of them is on Facebook or LinkedIn. I'll just have to wing it, I guess."

"Sometimes that's the best way. If you go into an interview thinking you already know some of the answers, it's easy to forget to ask some important questions. Facebook might tell you someone was born in Cincinnati, for example, but it doesn't say 'in the back of a cab on the way to the hospital'. There's no substitute for a solid interview."

"Like Porsche," she says, "there is no substitute."

"And practice," I say, picking up my ball and glove from the front porch.

"Do you mind if we do something a little different tonight?" she asks.

I notice she's still in jeans, not sweats, and hasn't taken her glove out of her car.

We've been playing catch every night, for at least an hour. We start about 15 feet apart, an easy game of toss and catch, then back up five feet every 10 minutes or so until we're throwing it the length of the backyard. I catch it more often than not and my throws are gradually getting a little more 'mustard' on them, as Tessa likes to say. My aim is still very iffy.

"Sure."

Maybe we're graduating to a bigger field. The backyard is only 60 feet across, which Tessa says is still 30 feet – 30 feet! – Shorter than the distance between two bases. I haven't picked up a bat, let alone swung at a ball, Tessa says we'll do some of that at practice tomorrow.

"Since we'll be practicing with the team tomorrow, can we skip practice tonight? Just this once? I haven't eaten yet today and I don't think I have the energy."

"Want me to order something in from Wok Inn or Skip the Dishes?"

I was very good with technology and my iPhone was loaded to the max with memory and apps.

"We can throw the ball a bit after that."

"I don't know, dude …"

First 'Stevie', and now 'dude'? What was going on here?

"Let's just hit the food court at the mall. I'll see how I feel after."

"Okay," I say, "you're the baseball boss. I'll drive."

***

"I like your car," she says of my coffee-colored 2016 Honda Civic as we pull up at the mall.

"It's reliable."

"Just like you."

I turn and look at her. What was THAT about?

"Do you have a name for it?"

"Um, no. Car?"

"How about Brown Sugar? You know, like the Rolling Stones song?"

"I've never heard it. My mom only listens to the Beatles. Don't the Rolling Stones worship the devil?"

"Oh you poor sheltered boy," she laughs. "Let's go in. I'm starving."

I'll be the first to admit it, malls and shopping aren't really my thing. Rick's, sure, but that was all neat sporting good stuff. The mall was mostly just … clothing stores. I hope nobody from work sees us.

My mom bought most of my clothing for me. I'm a 42 chest, 32 inseam and 16-inch neck. I take a size 10 shoe. It isn't uncommon for me to come home and find a bunch of new clothing laid out on my bed. Yes, even underwear. Men's medium boxer briefs.

Sometimes stuff fits great off the rack, sometimes not so much. Luckily, all it takes to make an oversize pair of pants functional is a belt. Comfort was key, fashion was not a concern. Other than I like my sweater vests and bowties. Always have, from the time I learned to tie them as a child.

"Let's split a pizza."

"I don't eat pizza. I don't eat anything mixed together. You get what you want. I'm not hungry. I'll have a Coke."
Which I sip through a straw, slowly, while Tessa regales me with a colorful account of her day at the homeless center. The pizza seems to be kicking in and she's soon percolating with untapped energy. I find myself enjoying listening to her talk. It's not what I'd call a two-way conversation, but it's … fun.
There's never a dull moment when Tessa's around. I smile.
"What?"
Oops. Busted.
"Nothing. Just admiring your multitasking abilities, you know, eating and talking at the same time. Literally," I laugh.
"One of my specialties," she laughs too. "You ain't seen nothing' yet."
She's staring at me, our eyes meet, and I look away.
"You know, I can probably help you in ways other than catching a baseball."
I raise my bushy eyebrows in response. I wish I could raise just one. I used to practice in front of the mirror, but never could get it quite right.
"Touché!' she laughs.
She'd set me up. And I took the bait.
"Okay, I'll bite. How can you help me?"
"I want to give you a fashion makeover."
Uh oh. Warning! Warning!
"You can keep the glasses, but everything else has to go. I'm sorry, did I hurt your feelings?"
Maybe coming from someone else it would, but not from her.
"Sure," I hear myself say.
What have I gotten myself into?

"You're not ready for the Mall of America yet, the big leagues, but I think we can find you some nice stuff here."

It's as if I'm putty in her hands? What happened to stuffy, stern Steve? Where is he when I need him?

"Where do you usually shop for clothes?"

"I don't."

"Well, you're not sitting here naked, so you must shop for clothes somewhere."

"My mom buys them for me. I don't try them on. I just wear what she buys me."

"Be still my heart," she says, putting a hand to her breast. "A man who will wear what he's told. Say it ain't so.

"Let's go," she says, jumping up from our table and grabbing my hand. Again.

I could get used to this hand-holding thing. It feels … good, somehow.

"So," she says, leading me to the Tommy store, why the bowties anyways? Some kind of tribute to Mr. Rogers?"

This girl wasn't shy. She was going to be a great journalist.

"Who?"

I'd never watched children's TV shows. Between school, work and my mom I was always too busy.

"It's a memory device," I say, feeling like I'm revealing one of my deepest, darkest secrets. "It helps people remember me. It's great for networking. 'Oh ya,' people say, 'the guy with the bowtie'. They remember me."

"And the eyebrows?"

"Same thing, just in case."

In truth, my bowties are like a child's security blanket. Because that's what I'd been when I started going to school and working with adults, a child. Bowties, sweater vests and the John Lennon glasses were a way to get people to take me seriously.

"Okay," says Tessa, "Fair enough. We all have our stuff. Things we're self-conscious about, ways of compensating. Take it from me. My mom's a clinical psychiatrist. I'm far more self-aware than I'd like to be. I swear I notice when I gain a single pound."

"You're not fat, Tessa."

"You're right, I'm not. But that's my 'thing', see? It's not necessarily reality, but it's MY reality."

I was starting to get it.

"Just like you don't really need to hide behind those bowties and bushy eyebrows. YOU might think you do, but you don't. You're the one making a big deal out of it, no one else. You're more than your bowties, Steve. You're smart, you have a good job, a nice home, good looking …"

Good looking? Did she just say 'good looking'?"

"People will remember you for you. Believe me."

She moves to stand directly facing me, about a foot apart. Too close. Much too close.

"For starters, let's get rid of this."

Her fingers brush my neck as she undoes my bowtie, sending a tingle down my spine. I never let anyone but my mom touch my bowties.

I wonder if she felt it too?

"Pick a change room," she says, "and I'll start bringing you clothes to try on."

She's back in what seems to me like an eternity but has only been five minutes.

"Here you go," she says, "try these."

She's brought a couple pairs of skinny jeans, some Dockers, a half dozen long-sleeved dress shirts, a couple of golf shirts and two blazers.

I've never been in a change room in a store before. I don't like it. Taking my clothes off in a little cubicle in a store ... who knew if they had two-way mirrors or hidden cameras. Someone could be watching me right now, I think, looking around the tiny box.

The clothes do look nice, though. And the first pair of pants I try on fit perfectly. I look at the tag. Dockers. I like these.

The skinny jeans ... do not fit. And they pinch in places I don't want to be pinched.

"Well?" I ask, stepping out of the change room.

"Turn around."

I turn around and when I'm facing her again, she's laughing.

"The pants are too small," she says.

"No kidding."

"And what's with the sweater vest?"

I'd put it on over one of the new shirts she picked out.

"Um..." I start to say.

"Okay. Try on the other pair of Dockers and lose the vest."

Wow. I liked the take-charge side of Tessa. That kind of mental toughness would serve her well, in journalism and in life.

I step out of the change room ... and am greeted by the sound of applause. Tessa, a couple of the young sales girls and one young sales guy are standing in a group outside the room, apparently waiting for me to emerge.

"Now THAT'S what I'm talking about!" says Tessa.

I'm blushing from the attention. I'm not sure I like it, maybe
...

"Like OMG," says sales girl one, "is this, like the same dude you came in with?"

"Nope," says Tessa. "That was the old Steve. Stevie. This is the new, self-confident, Steve. A man. Not a boy."

"I'll say," gushes sales girl two, pretending to fan herself and earning a sidelong glance from Tessa. "He's hot!"

She's right. I DO feel more self-confident. More … adult. And I look … good. At least these girls seem to think so.

And so does Tessa. I think.

I wonder what her boyfriend, the one who sent her those flowers, thinks about us playing catch together every night. Did she take him shopping like this too?

 "Now," she says, "let's get home and take care of those things you call eyebrows!"

Chapter 18 — Tessa

Wow!

There's definitely something there. I'm not sure quite what, when I accidently touched Steve's neck while undoing his bowtie. He flinched. I noticed, but didn't say anything. Poor guy was already way out of his comfort zone just going to the mall.

And then when I stood in front of him and trimmed his eyebrows. It was just some basic landscaping, but there was something almost ... intimate ... about it. It takes a lot of trust to let someone near your eyes with a pair of scissors.

And I've never seen such deep blue eyes, ever. Even on phony Hollywood types. Or Anna.

Those sales girls are right. Steve was looking h-o-t. Thanks to me. You're welcome, ladies. I think.

It's the least I could do for him.

Sure, we're still doing the playing catch, thing. But that's actually kind of fun. It definitely feels like I'm getting the better end of our deal.

***

Steve was right. There IS a deeper story here that needs telling.

The names Jenny gave me turn out to be incredible stories in themselves.

Micah, a 17-year-old 'street kid' has been on his own for three years already. Jenny's only known him for the past year.

He sometimes stays at the Osborne's, she says, when there's no room at the shelter.

When I ask where he lived before that, she simply replies, "You'll have to ask him."

So I do.

Micah has a lengthy history of run-ins with the law. Mostly misdemeanors for vandalism and petty theft.

The vandalism is mostly 'tagging', spray painting graffiti on various surfaces around town, like bridge decks and building walls. Garbage bins.

For Micah, the tagging serves as an outlet for both his creativity and his aggression towards authority.

That's how I imagine my mom saying it, anyways.

The authority that wasn't there for him as a child. The system that left him in a violent situation until he was old enough to flee. He has very little respect for the law. The cops had been to his home plenty of times, he told me, and done nothing.

The petty theft was at grocery stores. Things like beef jerky and granola bars. Red Bull.

He looks tough on the exterior, dresses the part in torn jeans and dark hoodie, his long, dark curly hair giving him an unruly, if not downright feral, appearance. He's had to adopt this persona, he says, to survive. In truth, he is unfailingly polite, at least to me. I have to ask him twice to call me Tessa and not ma'am.

The thing is, he's basically a good kid who the universe has conspired against.

What would I have done in his place? Would I have had the courage, at 14, to strike out on my own?

Micah had felt like he didn't have a choice. It was leave or die. He left.

"I have something for you," he says at the end of our interview, pulling a sketch pad out of his worn backpack.

There's a drawing on the last page, which he carefully tears out of the pad and hands to me.

"I did it the other day. When you were touring around with Mrs. Osborne. It's you. I hope you don't mind."

It. Was. Me.

A charcoal sketch, of me.

"It's beautiful, Micah. Thank you," I whisper, giving him a hug.

***

Doris is a white-haired, matronly-looking 71-year-old who, according to Jenny, is her 'right hand gal'.

Doris does a little of everything around the center – vacuums, cleans bathrooms, cooks and often just sits and talks with folks to keep them company or plays board games with them.

"A lot of these people just want someone to talk to for a few minutes," she tells me.

As before, however, the story isn't really WHAT Doris does at the center, but WHO she is and WHY she does it.

Doris' boyfriend had been drafted into the army at the age of 18 and sent to Vietnam. He arrived back home, just two months later, in a flag-draped wooden box.

"He was one of the lucky ones," she says. "At least he came back."

It was 1969. The summer of love.

Doris was a talented singer/songwriter in the Janis Ian or Joanie Mitchell vein. Folksy, pretty in that flower-child way and easy to listen to, but with a message.

Doris didn't like the war. No, she hated it. But instead of joining the protests, she joined a traveling USO group – she'd even met Bob Hope once – flying to bases around the world to bring a little bit of 'home' to wherever the troops were stationed.

She knew that for some of those boys, and many were still boys, this could be the last song, maybe the last female voice, they ever heard.

It was hard, she said, to look out into the audience knowing some of those faces would never make it home. Some wouldn't even make it to the end of the week.

So she gave it her all, every single time.

"It might not be the last performance of my life," she says, "But it might be the last performance of theirs."

"Can you play something for me?" I ask at the end of our interview.

Both Micah and Doris have courage that makes me ashamed I've ever complained about anything in my life. The truth was, is, I had, have, it pretty darn good compared to a lot of other people.

"Let's see if anybody's around," she says. "If not I guess you get a private show."

She grabs her guitar out of a case in the corner and we head out to the lounge area.

An indigenous couple sitting by themselves in a corner of the room move to the middle when they see Doris with her guitar. Music bridges all cultures.

She starts strumming, slowly, quietly, and then a bit louder. I think I recognize the song, it's not on my dad's playlist, but it should be.

And then she starts singing and I recognize it Bob Dylan's blowing in the Wind.

***

This week has flown by. Between doing interviews, calling to ask more questions and fact check, and writing everything up – not to mention my regular job duties – I've been a very busy girl. Plus, I'm still meeting Steve at his place to play catch every evening.

Honestly, I think he's about as good as he's going to get without actually playing. I'm having too much fun to tell him though.

So far, I haven't met his mom. Even though I'm pretty sure I caught her peeking out her bedroom window at us once. I'm sure I saw the blinds move.

"Is your mom's name Gladys?" I asked jokingly, making an obscure reference to the nosy neighbor in the old Bewitched TV series, Gladys Kraits. He didn't get it, of course. He hadn't watched hours of reruns with his dad like I have.

"No, it's Mary," he replies, deadpan.

I laugh. Now THAT'S my Steve.

MY Steve is also ultra-reliable, so I'm surprised when I arrive Friday evening to play catch and Brown Sugar, his loyal Honda Civic sidekick, is nowhere to be seen. I check my cell phone but there are no texts or voice mails. Interesting.

I'm about to call him when a knock on my passenger side window startles me. There's a lady smiling in at me... and she's got Steve's sky blue eyes.

I push the button and open the passenger side window.

"Stevie's running late," she says, sticking her head in to the shoulders.

Again with the 'Stevie'.

"I'm his mom, Mary. Stevie says to tell you he got called into a last minute meeting and for you to come in and wait. He'll just be a few minutes, he says. Meeting with that nice Mr. Osborne about some big feature story project."

My project.

Oh well, might as well meet the mom. Let's see what, if any, insights she can give me on just what makes Stevie, I mean Steve, tick.

Plus, I hadn't seen the interior of the house yet and was, what? Eager?

"Sure," I say, climbing out of my car and walking to follow her through the gate and up the walk to the front door.

"I just made some peanut butter cookies. They're Stevie's favorite, but he won't miss a couple." She turns and winks at me. "I'm not able to do much these days, but I can still bake. I just don't move around too well. I'm really happy to finally meet you. Stevie's never had a girlfriend before, you know."

"Oh, we're not …"

"Watch your step dear," she says at the threshold, "I always have trouble with that step. Stevie says he's going to put in a ramp."

There's a wheelchair folded up beside the front closet.

I stop and stare, dumbstruck.

"Come on in dear, I don't bite."

The inside of the house is … new. Everything. Open floor plan. Hardwood and tile floors. Solar tubes flooding the room with natural light. Stone hearth and fireplace. Nice. Very nice.

We go into the kitchen. Granite countertops. Shaker-style cabinets. Stainless steel appliances.

This is the newest old house I've ever been in.

"Nice, Isn't it?" she says, noticing my ongoing home inspection. And gaping mouth, no doubt.

"Oh, sorry," I say. "I'm just … I don't know. It's just not what I was expecting."

"We wanted a new home, one with modern appliances and such, but we didn't want to move way out to the burbs. We like our little house in our old neighborhood. So Stevie renovated it all. He did the floors himself."

"Really, I didn't know he was a handy guy."

"Oh yes, he's really good with his hands."

Too much information, or TMI, as Suzi would say.

And it didn't stop there. For the next 45 minutes, Mary gives me the Coles Notes version of Stevie's – now I'm doing it! – Steve's life story. Deadbeat dad, sick mom, childhood prodigy, no friends, the whole shebang.

I find myself feeling sorry for him, yet at the same time proud of him for what he's accomplished. I can sure understand how his mom is proud of him. And look at what good care he takes of her!

I wonder if I'd do the same for mine. I wonder if she'd even let me? Probably not without psychoanalyzing my inner motivations.

Speaking of psychoanalysis, I wonder if Steve's ever had any. Probably as a child. Probably poked and prodded and tested until he was sick of it if the formidable emotional defenses he's erected – far more formidable than a bowtie – are any indication.

Despite my initial reluctance, I'm enjoying myself, listening to Mary's stories about Steve to a background soundtrack of the Beatles Love album.

"I used to play guitar,' she says. "But I can't anymore. Not with these hands. I can still sing though. Stevie plays guitar and I sing along. He sings too, sometimes, but I think he likes to just listen to me. I used to play guitar and sing him to sleep as an infant, so he knew all the words by the time he was three or four."

Yet another side of the mysterious Steve Sondergaard.

"Stevie says he's going to take me one day," she says, as I start humming along to a very spacey version of Here Comes the Sun. "To the Cirque du Soleil show in Las Vegas."

Steve calls. His mom, not me. He's going to be at least another hour, putting tomorrow's paper 'to bed'.

"Speaking of 'bed'," I say, "I'd better get going. I've got to work tomorrow and you know how my boss feels about tardiness," I wink. "Thanks for the cookies and conversation. It was nice."

I know she goes to bed early, that I'm keeping her up, but I don't want her to know that I know.

I think. If that makes any sense.

"It was about time we met," she says as I get up. I notice she uses both her arms to rise from her chair.

She gives me a big hug at the door.

I can't remember the last time my mom hugged me.

I used to wish my dad wouldn't hug me so often. Now I'm not so sure.

"You two have been dating for how long now? A couple of weeks?"

"We're not ..."

Ah what the heck, she's so happy.

"Thanks Mrs. Sondergaard ..."

"Mary."

"Thanks Mary. It was great meeting you! Have a good night."

Chapter 19 — Tessa

We're at the karaoke bar. Steve and I.

He's never sang in public before. Heck, he's never even BEEN to a karaoke bar before.

He's hesitant, he's only ever sang along to Beatles songs at home. With his mom.

"Okay, do it for your mom," I say.

My guess is he's going to butcher 'Yesterday' or go for a Ring tune, those are usually fun and you don't have to be as good a singer. Maybe Yellow Submarine. Sorry Ringo. You're still the coolest Beatle.

Steve heads to the stage and he's looking good. He should be, I dressed him, black jeans and all.

Nobody's really paying attention. They're all either eating, or talking, or both.

Perfect. Don't want him getting too embarrassed.

And then I hear it. The opening piano notes to Let It Be. A long, slow song. Oh no, no Steve, I think, panicking for him. Pick something shorter, faster. By a worse singer.

He starts singing. And everything else in the bar stops.

People look up. Conversations stop. Heads turn.

Steve is singing the first verse of Hey Jude and He. Is. Perfect. If he was playing bass left-handed and had those droopy puppy dog eyes he could be a young Paul McCartney. He is THAT good.

Girls want to be with him, men want to be him, good.

So, maybe this wasn't such a good idea after all, this bringing him out of his shell idea. I wouldn't want it to go to his head, after all. Besides, I'm definitely not crazy about the way that redhead is looking at him. Hey, ginger, that's my man!

Maybe she'll get the message once I've done my song. I'm up next.

Born to be Wild.

That's me, and you better stay away from my man, red.

I can tell Steve's loving it, and as I finish he's there at the side of the stage to meet me.

Until I snag a heel, that is, (stupid heels, I never wear heels!) and do an unplanned stage dive … right into his arms.

His strong arms. Stronger than I expected, making me feel what? Safe? Secure? It feels … good.

"I thought you couldn't catch", I say, looking up at him, smiling, I hope invitingly.

He bends to kiss me as I lean my face up, anxious for that first touch of his lips on mine, and …

"Don't go breaking My heart."

I wake up to my alarm blasting out the '70s hit by Elton John & Kiki Dee.

"Daaad," I moan, pulling the pillow over my head.

He's always messing with my play lists.

And it was all just a dream.

A good dream, about Steve.

Chapter 20— Steve

"You told my mom WHAT?!" I practically yell at Tessa as we drive to our final team practice before the tournament.

"I didn't tell her we 'WERE' dating. I just didn't tell her we weren't. Apparently she's jumped to her own conclusions. You wouldn't have anything to do with that, would you?"

"Me?! I haven't told her anything. Except about working on your project. And about going to the mall. And about what a great baseball player you are. And … maybe I have been talking about you quite a bit lately. But I have not, NOT, told anyone you are my girlfriend."

"Are you saying I'm not girlfriend-worthy? That I'm not good enough to be your girlfriend?"

"No, no, for goodness sake, Tessa. I haven't told anyone you're my girlfriend, you haven't told anyone I'm your boyfriend. Nobody's told anybody anything. Okay?"

"Sure," she says, laughing. "I'm just jerking your chain. Your mom's nice. Other than the girlfriend thing."

She smiles at me and I can't help but laugh.

"Yup, other than that," I say, opening the trunk and pulling out my baseball equipment bag and throwing it over my shoulder. Tessa's got a smaller athletic bag containing just her glove, a ball and shoes. I like the way her pony tail sticks out the back of her ball cap.

The rest of the team is already here and good-naturedly throw a variety of greetings our way – some repeatable and some not.

"Steve-o!"

"The Designator!"

It's Mickey, from graphics. Our team captain. A pretty good guy and a pretty good player. He went out of his way to make sure he was the first to personally welcome each player to practice.

I make note of the effect it has on people, just to be welcomed and appreciated, and vow to incorporate it into my everyday dealings at the office.

"Hey y'all."

I'd recognize that phony southern drawl anywhere. Anna.

"Guys, you all know Anna," says Mickey warmly. "Nancy had to drop out and Anna volunteered to take her spot. Thanks Anna."

"Thanks Anna", we all mumble in unison.

"You're welcome, y'all."

And then to me, "I saw y'all at the mall the other night. You and Tessa. Are y'all a, you know, a thing?"

"We're just ..." I start to say.

What were we?

"Okay, let's play ball!" yells Mickey, saving me. His timing is impeccable. "Everybody take your position. Tessa you take second. I'll take short. Morty, you're pitching, of course. Paul you take first. Anna you're rover and Steve, Steve you're out in right field. Sound good?"

Paul works in advertising, but didn't want to play for them.

"They take it too seriously," he tells me, flashing a huge grin. "This will be more fun."

"Sounds good," I say, to no one in particular and start jogging out to my position.

"Well?" says Anna, jogging alongside me.

"No comment."

"I knew it!" she shrieked, somehow completely void of accent.

"No comment," laughs Tessa, jogging up on the other side, laughing. "Quick thinking, braniac. Now we're even."

"Tessa and Steve-o sitting in a tree," Anna begins singing. Things go downhill from there.

Turns out, catching a ball hit at around 70 miles per hour, 100 feet into the air, is a lot different than catching a ball thrown directly at your glove at about half that speed from about 30 feet away.

I lose the first few pop flies Mickey hits my way against the clouds and just cover my head with my glove until I see the ball land. One ball lands so close to me the 'thud' on the ground makes me jump. I hope they aren't counting on me to catch any pop flies.

Now he's hitting a few on the ground. 'Grounders', Tessa calls them, although we never practiced picking them up. Mickey hits a few to the infielders and then starts working his way around the outfield.

Anna makes no attempt whatsoever to retrieve anything – in fact, I think she might be filing her nails –so, after the first non-effort, Mickey shrugs his shoulders and hits one my way. Hard.

I wish I could be that mellow, I think, as the ball goes bounding past me.

"Steve! The ball!"

It's Tessa.

"Right. Got it."

I run to retrieve it and throw it in to Tessa, who's come out into field a little. She's got her glove up, giving me a target. THIS I can do!

I throw the ball in and Mickey hits another one out. I bend down and it goes between my legs and under my glove.

"Way to go, Buckner!' I hear Paul yell from first.

I have no idea what he's talking about. What's a 'Buckner'?

"You have to go down to one knee on those, Steve. Get your body in front of it."

It's Tessa. Still helping. But that sounds like it could hurt.

I grab the ball and throw it in again.

Mickey hits another one out to me and I get down on my knees, early, so it won't go by me.

Thump!

The ball takes a bounce and hits me squarely in the solar plexus, knocking all the wind out of me.

I can't breathe. This must be what dying feels like. The ball has hit my heart and stopped it and I'm dying. Right here on the field.

I open my eyes. I'm staring straight up, looking into the concerned faces of my teammates, who've gathered in a circle around me.

"Tessa," I gasp, "tell my mom I love her."

"Tell her yourself later tonight," she chirps back. "You just had the wind knocked out of you."

I ask her to drive me home, just in case.

"Okay, we need to go to Plan B," Tessa announces on our drive home.

"Plan B?"

"Trust me. And plan C, D and E too. Just in case."

"I do," I say. "I will."

"Okay, here's the plan."

Chapter 21— Tessa

It's tournament Sunday, and the plan, or, rather, plans, plural, are working. So far.

We're actually in the finals of this crazy tournament, thanks in part to a seeding round that forced the two powerhouses, Advertising and the Pressroom, to play early on the same side of the tournament brackets.

That meant someone from our side of the bracket had to get in, and it's us!

We'd squeaked out a win in our last round robin game thanks to a seventh inning run by Paul. We only played seven inning games, so Paul left his heroics for the end – and what an end it was.

We're down one run. We're also down to our last batter. There's no stealing allowed, but Paul's dancing off and on third base like it's a red ant hill. I've literally never seen anything like it. My mom would have diagnosed him with Restless Foot Syndrome for sure.

Most people avoid the rundown. The odds are stacked against you. Big time.

Even though he can't steal, instead of just pitching the ball to the batter, the pitcher, I guess trying to be a hero – and no doubt distracted by Paul's annoying antics – spins around and throws to third base.

He'll get Paul out instead, teach him a lesson for being such a jackass.

Except Paul was a jackass with his own plan.

People had underestimated him, thought he was just the class clown, most of his life – and he'd used it to his advantage. Just like he did on the field today.

The second the pitcher pivots, before the ball even leaves his hand, Paul is off towards home like he's shot out of a cannon. I've never seen a man that big move that fast. Except on TV.

The pitcher's committed to the throw, physically, but sees Paul moving and jerks his arm at the last instant in a vain attempt to pull his throw back. The movement causes the ball to come out high and it sails high over the third baseman's head.

Paul slides into home anyways. That's just how he rolls.

"They don't call me 'The Pollinator' for nothing!"

Pollinator? Pollinator? Hmm, depending on the spelling, one could take that a couple of different ways.

"I was a phys ed major, you know," he tells me back on our bench.

He'd talked his way into a sales job.

Hmm. Maybe if this Steve thing doesn't work out …

***

Heading into the finals, Steve and I are quite happy with how our own plans – we're calling them commandments – are working.

Plan A, Steve actually being able to play, went out the window at practice yesterday.

Plan B is having Steve stand way back in field and let everything fall in front of him, then just run up and grab it. Hold them to a single or double.

"Just don't let it go over your head," I say, "and you'll be fine."

"Maybe it won't come to me," he says.

That's the spirit.

Plan C, anytime Steve gets the ball he's to throw it to me and only me. Always.

Plan D, when up to bat, don't swing at anything. Ever.

Plan E, swing if you feel like it.

I know, Plan E contradicts the 'thou shalt not swing' rule in Plan D, but what the heck, if a perfect one comes down the pipe, take a swipe at it I tell him.

So far, he's come up to bat twice in each of our three prior games. He swung at one pitch per at bat, missed them all by a mile, was called out four times and walked twice, for an on-base percentage of .333. Baseball is a game of numbers and so far our numbers were adding up nicely.

Our pitcher is Morty, a 60-something-year-old Features Editor who's been around, he says, "since the days of hot lead typesetting."

Whatever that is. I'll have to remember to Google it when I get home.

I assume it means forever. For sure he's older than my parents, every person's definition of old. Your parents are old. When – if – you reach their age, THAT'S when you'll be old.

With his protruding beer belly and sad, seemingly permanently bloodshot eyes, Morty doesn't look like much on the ball field (or anywhere else, for that matter). Until he pitches. He has a way of putting perfect backspin on the ball so that when he tosses it, it literally comes straight down over the plate from about 10 feet up and is deceptively hard to hit. If you do hit it, it's about 90 per cent that's its going to be a pop-up. I've NEVER seen a ball spin like that. It's quite mesmerizing.

I found that out in practice, whiffing on a few before finding my timing and popping a few up.

It certainly IS amusing watching the big boys from the other departments corkscrewing themselves into the ground as they swing too hard, too fast, on pitch after pitch.

I'm a little embarrassed for them, almost. But not much. It kinda looks good on them.

Does that make me a bad person? Not on the ball field, baby.

I always like to surprise people in the first inning. Show them how it's going to be.

I love watching the looks on their faces, especially the guys. It makes some of them – not many, unfortunately – respect you, and some of them, too many, try even harder to be better than you.

It's a testosterone thing. My mom would explain it better than me, I'm sure. Genetic imperative and all that crap. Blah blah blah.

Advertising, our sworn mortal enemies – are up to bat first. Morty strikes out the first one – "Way to go Mor-ti-mer!" – yells Mickey, and gets their second hitter to pop up to shallow outfield – right where Anna would be if she was actually paying attention instead of taking endless selfies. I can imagine the caption: "This is me playing baseball." This is me barfing.

Now there's a runner on first. Perfect double play opportunity.

Morty knows it. He nods at Paul, then at me. He's going to try to get them to hit a grounder.

I'm positioned between first and second and take a couple steps closer to second base. I have to be able to get there turn the double. I'm ready.

And it's coming right to me. Hard.

The ball hits a bump in the infield and takes a hop to my right. I instinctively dive for it, grabbing the ball, rolling and getting up again all in one motion. Luckily, the move has brought me closer to second. I step on the bag, pivot and fire the ball to first. On a rope.

Whap! The ball hits Paul's big first baseman's glove and sticks there.

Double play. Three up, three down. Just. Like. That.

They have their own three up, three down inning, we have another, and we're into the bottom of the second before I get my first at bat. The way this is going, I may only get a couple of at bats. I better make it count.

One good thing about my lack of physical stature, I have a small strike zone. Pitchers have to make a pretty good pitch to get it in there, and if they do ... bam! To the moon Alice!

"Move in," says the Advertising pitcher, a swarthy-looking salesman named Tony.

"She can play," I hear one of the outfielders yell.

"I got this," yells back Tony. "Move in."

This is going to be fun.

I watch the first pitch come in, to get a feel for the height, the speed, the spin.

"Strike one," calls the umpire.

"Nice pitch," I say.

Tony just smirks.

I take the next pitch too, it's not bad, but it's a little outside and I have short arms. Short, but powerful.

"Ball one!" says the ump.

Like Goldilocks and the three bears, the next pitch is just right. Right. In. My. Sweet spot.

I drop my shoulder, transfer my weight and swing from my core.

Bink! There's a sound an aluminum bat makes when you hit the ball square, and that's it.

I round first as their fielder turns and runs to chase the ball that's gone over his head. Paul and Mickey are going to score. I'm holding up at second.

We've got two down and Steve's up next, but we're up 2-0. It stays that way for most of the game. A rare slow pitch pitcher's duel. Tony was a macho jerk, but he was good, I'll give him that.

Going into the top of the seventh and final inning, we're still up by two runs. Morty is nearly unhittable, and when they do hit it, our defense is solid.

Tony's up first, tags a grounder down the third base line and legs it out into a double. He's in scoring position on second.

The temptation to trash talk him as I stand next to him on second is hard to resist. But I do, even though he smells like garlic.

Morty strikes out the next batter and now their fielder is up, Jack, the one who I hit the ball over.

I know he's itching for revenge. He's going to try to really crank it.

"Get ready fielders," I yell. "Get ready Steve-o. Play's to me."

Morty pitches. I watch it arc, ever so gracefully, right up to the point where Jack launches it into orbit.

Or what must seem to Steve like orbit.

So much for hoping it didn't come to him.

Tony is holding up on second. Even though its Steve out there, Tony can't take the risk he might catch it. Jack is standing between first and second, watching, waiting.

It's right to him. You don't even have to move, Steve. Just get that glove up, get that glove up …

He does, but a fraction of a second too late, and a fraction of an inch to the side. The ball hits his glove, sticks … for a second … and then rolls off the end of his glove, hitting his foot before coming to rest on the ground.

He drops it. Tie game.

"Steve-o! Steve-o!"

It's rude Tony, chanting derisively. No one else from their team is joining in.

Steve throws the ball in and hangs his head. I don't have to look at him to know there are tears in his eyes. This means so much to him. Not to win. But to be accepted, to be valued as part of the team.

Morty strikes out the next two batters and we're up next. One last at bat in a tie game.

It's déjà vu as both Paul and this time Morty are on base ahead of me. Paul on a big hit, Morty on a walk.

Tony's not too happy about it. He didn't want to walk Morty and he can't walk me to get to Steve, in the lineup behind me. It's against the rules to deliberately walk a female player.

Paul is dancing off and on second base like it was made out of hot coals. Maybe his shoes are too tight. Whatever the case, he promised to bring the 'fun' and he's certainly delivered. I'd just about pay to watch this guy play.

At the plate, I'm expecting Tony's best 'stuff', if he has any. I guarantee he'd love nothing better than to put me in my place for 'girling' him with that earlier hit.

Instead, he hits me with the pitch.

He hit me.

I'm still standing in the batter's box.

He hit me. He threw it right at me. I can't believe it. In a company slow pitch game.

Normally, I'd move out of the way, but it was so unexpected, so … low – even for Tony – that I just froze.

Rather than risk having me bat Morty home, he hit me. Probably it had more to do with me not embarrassing him again and less to do with whether we got the run or not.

Tony was only looking out for himself, even if it cost his team the game.

I took a couple steps towards the mound, still holding the bat … and he flinched. He thought I might come after him – and he was scared. He should be.

Someone grabs my sweater from behind.

"Don't worry about it, Tessa!"

It's Steve.

"We've got them right where we want them."

That's debatable. We're tied in the bottom of the last inning of the championship game, there's two away, the bases are loaded, and Steve's up.

Mighty Casey jokes aside, we're in trouble.

Time for drastic measures.

"Thanks," I say, handing him the bat. "Plan D."

"Plan D?"

"Plan D. No matter what. Plan D. Trust me."

"I do."

Those words are starting to have a nice ring to them.

Steve may not be able to hit, but he's got plenty of patience and can take pitches with the best of them.

And he's coachable. I like that in a man.

True to plan, Steve plants his feet, gets his grip, crouches slightly, bat cocked over his right shoulder … and watches ball after ball go by without moving a muscle.

"Is this guy for real?" says Tony. "Hey ump, he's got to swing at the good ones."

"Maybe I will," I can hear Steve say from my locale on first base, "If you throw any."

Ooh. Burn. I like it.

The count gets to three and two, full count, three balls and two strikes – something's got to give on the next pitch, one way or another.

The pressure's all on Tony. He has to throw a strike or he walks Steve and we win. If he strikes Steve out, we still have a chance in extra innings.

Here we go. Tony brings the ball back, whips his arm back forward and releases the ball.

It passes right through the middle of the strike zone as Steve stands motionless as an Easter Island statue.

Oh no. A perfect strike.

Steve looks at me and our eyes meet in silent resignation. He trusted me and I let him down. That's how I feel.

"Ball four! Batter take your base."

"What?!" yells Tony, throwing his glove in the dirt on the pitcher's mound. "You've GOT to be kidding?!"

Classy, as always, Tony.

"The ball didn't arc six feet. It has to arc," says the ump evenly, "it didn't. It went over the plate but didn't arc. Ball four."

Game, set and match. We win!

Tony stomps on his glove. Yes, Tony, it's the glove's fault, not yours.

This guy's a real piece of work. I'll bet his mommy's REAL proud.

Meanwhile, Steve, all smiles now, begins walking to first base as the rest of the team comes running off the bench to crowd around home plate. They're waiting for Morty to come home.

I run down the first base line to meet Steve and he's surprised to see me. He thinks we need to round the bases. Sweet, silly Steve.

"Tessa, what are you …"

"We won Steve!" I yell, leaping up to hug him around the neck and wrapping my legs around his waist. "You don't have to go to first. It's over. We win. Morty just has to touch home plate."

I give him a quick kiss. Just a peck.

He swings me around in the air, one complete revolution, my feet now flailing six inches above the ground as he twirls me. His arms ARE strong, just like in my dream.

"C'mon," I say, my feet back on solid ground and head in the clouds. "Let's go meet Morty at home plate!"

Morty, meanwhile is walking home slowly. Very slowly. He even stops to crack open a post-game beverage … looking directly at Tony as he takes a large swallow, and then belches. It's Morty's moment, and he's savoring it.

It's OUR moment too. Mine and Steve's. We did it! We. Did. It.

"Yes!," I yell as Morty delicately places one big toe on the plate, officially sealing the victory.

Mickey breaks into an impromptu version of Queen's 'We Are the Champions' and the rest of us join in. We don't know all the words, so it's just the chorus, over and over. We're horribly out of tune – except Steve, I notice – but it sounds … so … perfect.

We won the tournament.

My project is in the final edits stage.

And I kissed Steve. I KISSED Steve.

And he kissed me back, a little.
I could get used to this pretend girlfriend/boyfriend thing.

Chapter 22 — Tessa

Faith Hill's song 'This Kiss' has invaded my brain.
Since yesterday.
THAT was a mistake.
The hug, sure, no problem. But why didn't I stop there? Why did I … kiss my boss?
Now everyone, not just Anna, thinks we're an item.
Not necessarily a great thing for my career.
Or Steve's, if it gets back to Mr. Osborne.
I don't want people thinking I got my job – if I'm even offered one – based on anything other than merit.
Oh well, it's probably over now. Whatever 'it' is. Was.
My project's just about done. We're about to meet to talk about it.
 He can kind of catch, sometimes, and the tournaments over.
I guess I won't be meeting him in the evenings anymore.
Unless he wants to go shopping, I laugh to myself.
I did help him with his wardrobe 'malfunction at the junction', that's for sure. I'm not so sure, however, whether that was for Steve … or for me. In the end, probably a win-win. I got to go clothes shopping with someone else's money, and he definitely looks better.
I notice Joan, a divorced and attractive 30-something-year-old reporter on the politics beat, help herself to a long look as Steve walked through the office to the coffee machine this morning.
Maybe I did it for Joan? I hope not.
What is this, jealousy? The green monster. That's crazy, we're just friends. Coworkers. Amigos. Comrades. Okay, maybe not comrades, that came with political connotations.

This is it, I think as I enter his office to discuss my project. My last week. Maybe. Probably.

There's been no mention of a possible job offer.

Nope, he doesn't really need me for anything now. No real reason for him to keep me hanging around. He can catch, sort of. He looks good. He must see how the other gals look at him. Plus, my internship is about to end.

And he's my boss.

My fake boyfriend boss. I'll explain things to a few people at the office next week, if I'm still around. Set the record straight.

Steve would have to talk to his mom. I hope she takes it okay.

I think of something she told me, and smile. She is SO proud of him.

"He's very muscular, you know," she told me. "It's from mowing all those lawns as a youngster and, of course, pushing his mother's wheelchair around."

I'd felt those arms lift me up and twirl me at the ball tournament.

I remember when I showed up at his house to throw the ball early one time. He answered the door in an apron and I laughed. I'd caught him doing the vacuuming and dusting. When he came out the back door to play the apron was gone, replaced by a black leather tool belt.

"Manly enough for you?" he'd queried.

It was.

"Yes, and it matches your glove," I quipped.

He threw his glove at me.

The memory brings a smile to my face as I enter his office.

One thing's for sure, I'm NOT going to mention the kiss.

"Good morning, Steve."

Chapter 23 — Steve

Monday morning is bittersweet.

Sure, we're the new champions, but what is that really worth?

It was great yesterday – but now, nothing.

Then there was 'the kiss'.

Best not to mention it. Pretend it never happened.

It was just a spur of the moment thing, after all.

Nope, it's back to business as usual today.

But it DID feel good. Her lips on mine. Her body next to mine. Her legs … I didn't think they were long enough to wrap around me. But they did. She did.

Is it getting warm in here?

I notice Paul come in to the department to say "good morning" to everyone, adding a special "Hi Anna" at the end.

Tony even stuck his head into my office earlier, looking for Tessa, but she wasn't in yet.

I wonder what THAT'S all about?

If I was him, I'd steer clear of that girl.

I probably should too, except I'm her boss.

And boyfriend, apparently, according to my mom … and Anna.

But not according to us. Tessa and I. At least, I don't think she feels that way.

I'm not sure what I'm feeling, something, maybe last night's glass of celebratory champagne.

I do know the final version of Tessa's project is due this week.

That's why we're meeting this morning. No other reason.

***

"Good morning, Steve."

 "Good morning, Tessa. Or should I say champ?"

Oh good, she's in business mode.

"About that kiss…" we both blurt at the same time, both of us stopping to let the other speak.

"I'm sorry," she says.

"It didn't mean anything," I say.

"Just the excitement of the moment," she says.

"Could happen to anyone," I say.

"It doesn't mean we're really boyfriend and girlfriend."

"No, no."

"it was just a little peck, nothing really."

"Nothing at all."

She looks a little disappointed.

I know I am.

Didn't she just say it was nothing?

I don't understand women at all. Not my mom, not Tessa, not any of them.

Seems to be a lot of feelings involved. A lot of unspoken communication that I was somehow supposed to pick up on.

It was nice to be back in the office. My happy place.

Where logic, and not feelings rule the day. And night.

"Let's get down to business."

And we do.

I have to hand it to her, she's done a great job.

Her eyes well with tears when I tell her.

I know how important this is to her.

I felt another hug coming on and regretted the desk between us, and the open office door.

"We don't always give bylines to interns," I say. "We usually go with 'Staff Writer'."

Odd, when you think about it, because, technically, interns aren't yet 'on staff'.

"But I convinced Mr. Osborne you deserve it on this one. It will make a great portfolio piece for you."

Not only did she do a great job on the story, but I have to admit she's done a good job on me too.

I can catch, sort of. At least I'm not afraid to try.

I'd like to learn to hit, but I guess that depends on Tessa. Whether she wants to teach me. Whether she's even still in town.

It's not just the baseball, though, I know.

Or the clothes.

I'm more confident. I've always been smart, but not confident. It's a powerful combination, to be smart AND have the self-confidence to express your ideas.

Of course, I AM a little more stylish. Hot, even, according to the girls at the clothing store. Of course, I know they say that to everyone, just to sell stuff. Like waitresses who flirt in hopes of getting a big tip.

I may be naïve to the ways of the world, but I'm not THAT naïve. Thanks to Tessa.

Still, I do like the way people look at me now. It's … different. Like I'm an actual grown-up now.

And this whole boyfriend/girlfriend thing, to make my mom happy … probably I could ask someone out, but who? I still only knew people from the office. One of the sales girls? I don't think so. I'm confident, but not THAT confident.

I could go online. But once they find out I live with my mom they'll be 'gonzo Alonzo'.

Another phrase Tessa's taught me.

Ah, yes, Tessa. My Mom still thinks SHE's my girlfriend.

Seems a lot of things in my life right now are thanks to Tessa.

We can't really be boyfriend and girlfriend, though, even if she wanted to … because I'm her boss.

Chapter 24 — Tessa

Great portfolio piece?!

The comment cuts like a double-edged sword.

So the piece is good, but not good enough that they are going to offer me a job?

Maybe there just isn't a full time position open.

Which means I'll need a portfolio to apply for other jobs. In other towns.

Steve has already gone to bat for me on the byline, but there's nothing he can do about hiring me if there isn't a position open.

I know there isn't a position in City, just another intern coming in once I leave.

"We have to present our concept to the Editorial Board this Thursday," he says, "So we've only got a couple of days to prepare. Tessa?"

I'm still mentally paused on 'portfolio'.

What did I have, really? Several dozen obituaries and a few advertorials. If my enterpriser doesn't run, I've essentially got nothing. Nothing impressive anyways.

We have to nail this presentation and my story has to run. The full two-page layout.

Steve has done all he can, it's up to the Board now.

"We'll walk through the presentation a couple of times," he says. "Figure out what you're going to say and what I'm going to say. So that we're in synch."

"Right," I say. Or else its bye, bye, bye Tessa.

"Then I guess we should put these boyfriend/girlfriend rumors to rest. I'll talk to my mom. You talk to Anna."

"Right."

I'd rather talk to his mom.

So this is how it's going to end. Me packing a box, a very small box, of my personal items a week from Friday and walking out the front door. Would I even see Steve again? Ever?

"Steve," I say, my eyes filling with tears and my voice cracking, "thanks."

I'd read lots of fake boyfriend romance books and they always ended with the main characters falling in love and living happily ever after.

Not like this. Not just … walking out the door. Was that how our story, mine and Steve's, was fated to end?

***

It's Thursday morning and Steve's at my desk. He seems panicked. For him.

"Tessa, I've got to go. I can't make our meeting."

I check the time. It's 9 and our presentation is at 10.

"I'm sorry. I've got to go. Sorry. It's my mom."

Oh, it's your mom. Why didn't you say so? This is only the rest of my life on the line here!

"Um …"

"Sorry." He gently touches the top of my hand with his. "I've got to go."

And he's gone. Just like that. Bye, bye, bye.

You know how in some cartoons there's a little angel is sitting on one shoulder and a little devil on the other, giving the character advice. That's me. It's like I'm a female Fred Flintstone in a cartoon version of Life of Tessa.

"Well, what did you expect," says the devil. "He's a mommy's boy. Always has been. Always will be."

That seems rather harsh, but even though I'm only 21, I've already met my share of mommy's boys. Men who can't let go of their mom's apron strings and the moms who dote on their, to them, perfect sons. Most of whom are far, far from perfect, in my humble opinion.

No girl would EVER be good enough for their sons and it's near impossible to compete with someone's mommy for their attention and affection. Not a winnable war and probably not a battle worth fighting.

For their part, the sons, overall, love their mothers, but often aren't above playing the sympathy card or laying the guilt on to get what they want. I've seen that work both ways, actually.

It seems to be largely a single-mom with one son at home thing – the sons are single because they're looking for a girl just like their mommy. It's just … strange.

"So he's nice to his mom," retorts the Angel perched on my other shoulder. I've always thought of my good angel as a bit of a smartass. "Is that a crime now? Would you rather he wasn't?"

I'm fine with him being nice to his mom, close even. Full disclosure: I'm probably a little jealous. My mom and I have all the closeness of a porcupine at a balloon convention. Translation: we're not that close.

She does know a lot about people, though. Sort of. I know she'll boil it down to clinical practitioner's terms, but if I read between the lines, like I always do, I might be able to glean some a couple of useful tidbits from her ramblings.

Ya, that's what I'll do. I'll ask my mom.

In the meantime I have exactly an hour, nope, 55 minutes now, after all the internal debate club members have their say, to prep for the biggest presentation of my life.

I think I'm going to throw up.

Thanks Steve. Thanks a lot.

***

I'm on time, but everyone else is already seated around the boardroom table. And they're all … old. Nobody's smiling. Serious news people never smile. What's up with THAT? Some of these people, I think as I scan the room for familiar faces, will be happy to go through their entire lives being grumpy. Being grumpy is literally what makes them happy. Their entire life is one big oxymoron.

Mickey gives me a smile and a nod. He's there representing the graphics team and is the only other person under 50. I can only imagine what HE thinks of these meetings. A necessary evil, I suppose, so that he can plot his layout strategy.

Mr. Osborne is there, at the head of the table, and gives me a discreet wink. It's reassuring to know he's in my corner. Since Steve seems to have other priorities.

They've left the seat at the other end of the table, the hot seat, and open for me. Awesome.

I pop open my laptop and connect it to the USB port on the boardroom projector.

"This is Micah," I begin, clicking on the arrow to launch the first video clip.

We'd done a complete 'day in the life' of both Micah and Doris. I followed them everywhere, for an entire day. I left Doris in her small condo after she cooked us a simple dinner of leftovers brought home from the homeless center.

"They'll just go bad if someone doesn't eat them," she'd said of the day-old sandwiches and soup.

I stuck it out with Micah the full 24 hours.

"I promise you nothing like this, nothing this in-depth, has ever been done at the Bulletin-Star," Steve had said. "Not by anyone."

He was impressed with the lengths I'd go to get the story, with my level of commitment. Most feature writers – certainly not Anna – would never dream of dressing in their dad's old clothes and pushing a shopping cart full of bottles around for a day. Then sleeping under some trees in a park. Thank God it wasn't winter!

Dean the cameraman wasn't too crazy about that last part, so I'd shot some nighttime footage on my iPhone. The quality wasn't great, but the images were real. Very real.

I tell the board about the main premise, the uniqueness of the angle, the raw emotion of the video and photos, and how we'd like a two-page space budget to run the feature as a DPS – double-page spread – in a sort of photo essay format.

Mickey's nodding his head and taking notes. Probably already building the layout in his head. Wait until he sees all the great photos!

Everyone else looks … the same as they did when I walked in. Stoic. Bored even. There's a couple of whispered comments exchanged, and a couple of shared glances but, other than that – nada. Nothing. I can't read these folks at all. I may have stumbled into a high-stakes poker tournament by mistake.

These people are so … so … emotionless.

"Well, any comments?"

It's Mr. Osborne, looking around the room, going from face to unblinking face, breaking the uncomfortable silence. My hero!

Nobody speaks. They're all waiting to see what the great and powerful Oz thinks before they reveal their opinions. What a bunch of brown-nosers.

"I just have one," he says.

And, getting to his feet, he begins to applaud.

Slowly at first, but then faster as everyone joins in.

They like it. They really like it.

I look at Mickey and he's positively beaming back at me.

"I knew you could do it, Tessa," he says, fist-bumping me on his way out the door.

We fist-bump now.

"Tessa."

It's Mr. Osborne. And, what's this? He's got his fist out, for a bump, I hope, so I do it.

"Great job."

And then, nodding after the other people now filing out of the room and lowering his voice, "Bunch of brown-nosers."

Chapter 25 — Tessa

Wow!

Talk about an emotional roller coaster.

My stomach has had more ups and downs in the past couple of hours than a yo-yo.

More ups and downs even than a Kardashian in an NBA locker room.

More ups and downs than, well, you get the picture.

When I arrive home this evening, it all comes gushing out. I know I'm opening myself up to my mom's critique – maybe I'm some sort of masochist (I wonder what Freud would say about THAT?) – But I can't help myself. When I'm nervous, or upset, or excited … or awake … I talk.

"Try not to take it personally, dear," she always says.

Not the easiest thing to do when someone's picking apart your life, but I'm desperate.

My mom and dad are both home and I spill my guts. About the shopping trips, playing catch, his mom, the dream, the kiss …

"You kissed him? I thought you were just friends," says my dad.

"So did I," I say.

"Hmm," says my mom, taking notes.

I tell them about me being his fake girlfriend to keep his mom happy … and about him pretending to be my boyfriend to … to what? To keep Anna happy? Why hadn't we nipped that one in the bud already?

No, I thought, it wasn't to keep Anna happy. Remember, Tessa, It was so YOU wouldn't have to explain the flowers. Steve did that for YOU. For me.

"Okay," says my mom.

She's ready to pronounce judgment.

I brace myself internally for what's to come. Most likely a pseudo-psychology lecture on how the little devil and angel are represented by the id and super-ego, the id representing our primal urges and the super-ego our conscience and logic. The ego, I know, mediates between the two extremes, helping keep one's behavior in check. Or so says Sigmund Freud.

That's it! All I need is a third angel to be my ego.

At least it wasn't all about sex this time. Freud seemed to have a somewhat unhealthy obsession with sex, in my opinion. Surely my mom didn't share ALL of his philosophies. No, definitely not.

I try not to think about it.

"According to Maslow's Hierarchy of Needs ..." my mom begins, surprising me.

She's not going to do Freud this time, instead she's gonna go full Maslow on me. Alright, bring it on.

Way back in 1943, Abraham Maslow had proposed that human motivation was based around a multi-tiered series of needs. At the bottom of the pyramid were the elements necessary for survival, basic needs like food, sleep, water and shelter. Next came belongingness and love needs and, at the top, for those lucky enough to get there – self-actualization. That was the icing on the cake of life.

"He simply doesn't need you dear. He's already got everything he needs."

"Thanks, Mom, you always know just what to say."

If you want to make me feel like a petulant child who's just been scolded.

Besides, NEED and WANT are two completely different things.

He might not need me, not in that way, not to survive. But did he want me?

It's not that my mom is overly critical or demanding, just that she's … emotionally bankrupt. She's listened to so many people's problems that they don't impact her anymore. She's developed a tolerance, no, an immunity, to the emotional pain of others. Even me.

For her, everything has to relate back to Maslow's theory or the human genetic imperative, the need to propagate one's genetic line. It was all about the science, not about … real human feelings.

Men do this, women do that.

If only it were that simple, I thought.

"Try not to think about it," are her words of wisdom.

"Thinking too much is dangerous. Our big human brains are our biggest strength AND our biggest weakness. Try not to think too much dear. It's not good for you. For me, yes. For you, no."

Not very scientific, or empathetic, or even nice, but probably some of the best advice she's ever given me.

If only I would take it.

If only I could take it.

"There is no try, only do," adds my dad, quoting Yoda from Star Wars.

"Fear is the mind killer, honey," he says, quoting from yet another sci-fi series, Dune.

"Of course it is, dear," says my mom, rolling her eyes at me.

"I saw that," says my dad.

Great. My mom quotes Freud and Maslow and my dad quotes hockey players and movie aliens.

I'm going to have to look elsewhere for advice.

I grab my cell phone and, heading to my bedroom, push Q on my speed dial app and call my ego, my third angel.

"Hey girl!"

"Hey Suzi. Got a minute?"

Chapter 26 — Steve

"I've got to go."

I hate to abandon her like this, an hour before our big presentation, but I have no choice. It would have to be her presentation now.

She's totally capable of handling it. I wish she had as much confidence in herself as I have in her.

Most interns wouldn't be able to handle it. Either the assignment OR the Editorial Board meeting. She'd nailed the story – stories – and, based on our dry-runs the past couple of days, knew the presentation inside-out.

She could do my part, no problem. Maybe better. It WAS her story, after all. And she'd literally lived it. I'm very impressed and so is Mr. Osborne.

"She's making you look good," he said to me earlier this morning.

More like we make each other look good.

If she stays cool, doesn't get excited and sticks to the script. Just stick to the script, Tessa, you'll be fine.

In any case, I have no choice. She HAS to do this for me.

It's nice to have someone I can count on. For a change. Right now, more than ever.

I'd bought my mom a Life Alert a few years back, one of those 'Help, I've fallen and I can't get up' pagers – which we'd been lucky enough not to need. Until today.

The company dispatcher called literally seconds ago to tell me my mom has fallen down the stairs.

Emergency medical assistance is on the way, but I want to be there. I need to be there. I'm all she has. She's all I have. We were all each other had ever had. Really.

Unless you count Tessa. Mom seems to like her. So do I, but ... there were so many 'buts'.

Like the fact I'm her boss. For now, anyways. There aren't any jobs open in City, so THAT was about to end. As far as I know, there aren't any jobs available at the paper at all. Not in Editorial anyways.

There WAS that kiss, but – again with the 'buts' – but that was a spur-of-the-moment baseball celebration thing. I'd seen that Mickey guy, the design team leader, sitting on the corner of Tessa's desk the following Monday, looking pretty chummy.

I know I can't get home before the ambulance leaves, so I head directly for the hospital.

"Sorry girl," I say to my car, Brown Sugar. "I'm going to have to drive you hard today."

Oh great, I think, stepping on the gas, now she's got ME doing it.

I arrive in time to meet the ambulance as it pulls in. My mom's pretty out of it from the painkillers and the medics have immobilized one arm. There's a bump and a cut on her forehead.

"Oh Stevie!" she cries upon seeing me. "I'm sorry dear."

Sorry for what? Falling?

"I didn't mean to make you miss your presentation today. I'm sorry."

So she HAS been paying attention.

"That's okay, Mom," I say, holding her good hand. "I'm here now."

"She took a nasty spill," says the closer of the two paramedics, a large African American with a shaved head and bulging biceps. "Found her at the bottom of the stairs."

His touch is surprisingly gentle for such a big man as they transfer her from the gurney to a bed.

"She's got MS," I say, by way of explanation.

"Saw the bracelet," he says, nodding at her wrist. "It might be time for one of those stair lifts."

Oh no. This was MY fault. If only I'd put that stair lift in. We'd talked about it, but I hadn't done it because ... because I was too busy throwing a baseball.

With Tessa.

Well, I'm pretty sure that isn't going to happen again.

She's moving on to bigger and better things, somewhere else.

I'm staying here, with my mom.

And I don't just mean the hospital.

***

"Hi Mom," I say, entering the room.

They're going to keep her an extra couple of days for observation, so I arranged for a private room with a TV. They set her broken wrist, but are worried about a possible concussion. Since I can't be with her 24/7 it's best to keep her in.

"Sign my cast?"

Apparently it's some kind of pop culture tradition and I notice she's got a few other names on there. Some with the prefix Dr. and some in pink with little hearts above the name. Nurses, I suspect, bless their souls. I find a blank spot and sign.

'Steve was here'.

"I'm so sorry Stevie," she starts to cry again.

"Sorry for what, Mom? Falling? That's my fault. I should have had that lift in by now. I shouldn't have spent all that time with ... throwing a stupid baseball."

"Sure you should have, honey. Look how much fun you had. And you made some new friends. And met a nice girl. Seeing you happy like that …"

And she's crying again.

Now's as good a time as any.

"It was never real, Mom. Between Tessa and I. We were never really boyfriend and girlfriend. We just let you think that to make you happy. I'm sorry. I didn't really lie, but … I'm sorry."

Now she's laughing. What kind of meds are they giving her?

"Oh I know that, dear. I've known it all along. I just thought I'd play along with your little game. String it out for a while, see if anything happened."

I can only imagine how stupid the look on my face is. Duh. Why is it kids think their parents are so dumb? She had it figured out right from the beginning. Quite possibly more than I did.

"Well, her project's done and there's no jobs at the paper, so it wouldn't have worked out anyways. It's probably for the best in the long run. Besides, we don't have room for a wife in our house."

"About that," she says, "I've been thinking …"

"Uh oh."

"No, no, not about you and Tessa, per se, but about the future. About your future. I'm holding you back."

There are tears in her eyes again.

"No you're not, Mom. I'm right where …"

"Right where you want to be? Here? In this town? In this house? With me? Forever? Forever's a long, long time, Stevie. And I saw your face when you were with Tessa. She might be the one. She might not. I like her. But, someday, eventually there will be 'the one'. You can thank me then."

Thank her? Thank her for what?

"I have an idea," she says.

I sit and listen. It's not bad. It might just work. And, by the time she's done explaining all the details, I'm sold.

"As for Tessa," she says, "don't do anything hasty. Take a step back if you want, but don't make any rash decisions you'll regret later. Regret's an awful heavy piece of baggage to carry around for the rest of your life."

I wonder what regrets she has. What kind of baggage she's carrying that she's sheltered me from all this time.

"I won't," I say, "it's not like we're breaking up. We never really were."

She looks like she's not sure if she believes me and I don't blame her. I'm not sure I believe me.

And if it is the fake break-up of a fake relationship ... why does it feel so real?

Chapter 27 — Tessa

"Hey Suzi. Got a minute?"

"I've got more than a minute. For you, sister, I've got all night. What's up?"

"It's about Steve."

"No kidding. Are you gonna go for it, or what?"

Ah Suzi, always so subtle.

"I … don't know."

Which was the truth, but sounded so … so high school.

"I'm not sure he feels the same way I do."

Which was what, exactly? I wasn't even sure I knew the answer to that question myself.

"Plus, they haven't offered me a job. Which means he won't be my boss."

"Which is good. "

"But which means I'll have to get a job somewhere else, out of town."

"Which is bad."

"Unless it's a good job."

"Back to good."

I give her my best 'frowning mom' look. Minus the eye roll.

"I heard that."

What? How?

"Just kidding," Suzi laughs. "Girl, I wish I had your problems. I mean OPTIONS."

Options, I think, what options?

"Options, what options?"

"OMG. What IS your problem, girl? You're like, 21 going on, like 100. Why worry so much so far into the future. You're both here, now. And that's all that matters."

"Ya, maybe …"

"Maybe?! Maybe?! You're in some serious denial there, girlfriend. Look how he went out of his way to help set you up with another feature story. He didn't have to do that. I've never seen him do it for anyone else."

"That's just because he needed to fill his newspaper section. He would have gotten someone else to do it."

"Uh huh. And he went to bat for you after that feces incident. He took full responsibility for that. Osborne gave him crap. I heard it."

"Can we please not refer to it as 'the feces incident'? It makes it sound like something else."

"I've seen the way he looks at you. The way you look at him. It's not just Anna who's noticed."

Anna. Grrrr.

"Aren't you tired of pretending he's your boyfriend? Don't you wish he really was? If you're not working here, he's fair game. Look at him. He's yummy. Someone's gonna scoop him up if you don't. Maybe even Anna."

No. Not Anna.

"He doesn't even like Anna."

"Maybe not. But I'm not sure that matters to HER. If she sets her sights on him, he's a sitting duck. Once she gets her hook set, she'll just reel him in. Nice and easy."

"Okay, enough with the hunting and fishing metaphors. He's not a duck, or a fish."

"Doesn't mean she's not angling for what he's got dangling."

"That's disgusting."

"Doesn't mean it isn't true."

 "Besides," I say, "he's never really asked me out."

"OMG. Seriously?! You're going to wait for HIM to ask YOU? Hello, 1950s, yes, Tessa's here if you're looking for her.

You're waiting for HIM to ask YOU? He's more likely to ask won't you be his neighbor. I mean, he looks different now, thanks to you, but he's still … Steve. You could be waiting a while. In the meantime …"

"Anna."

"He may not like her, now. But he's a man. And to girls like Anna, it's like shooting fish in a barrel. I say go for it. What have you got to lose? Maybe they offer you a job, maybe they don't. Maybe you leave town, maybe you don't. Maybe it takes a while. Who knows? My point is, stop worrying so much about tomorrow and try to enjoy today. You're only 21, there will be lots of tomorrows."

Wow. That's Suzi for you. She tells it like it is. Considering she's the same age as me, lives in the same town – also with her parents – and is also single, she's pretty wise to the ways of the world.

She says it's from watching The Bachelor, but I have my doubts.

"Ya," I say, somewhat hesitantly, "Maybe … Hey what are you doing for dinner tonight? Tonight is Tex/Mex night and my dad's cooking 'Delgadillo tacos'. He's combining his egg thing with ground armadillo meat and taco sauce. Apparently they eat armadillo in Texas."

"They eat anything that sits still long enough for you to shoot it in Texas," laughs Suzi. "Sure, see you in a bit. Wouldn't miss it for the word. Delgadillo tacos! I might be falling in love with your dad."

OMG. KMN. TMI.

"Or at least his cooking. Can't wait for the roast buzzard at Christmas. "

"And THAT'S another thing! Did you know Steve doesn't eat any mixed foods?"

"Hmm. No Chinese food? No Italian?"

"He doesn't even use sauce. On anything. Unless you count ketchup. And even then he'll only eat Heinz."

"Heinz is good."

"He doesn't even like the food on his plate to touch. His mom's spoiled him."

"Okay, so let me get this straight. You don't want to go out with Steve, even if you stay in town, because he's a fussy eater who's nice to his mom? Do I have it right?"

"That's about right," I sigh, realizing the absurdity of it all. "See you in a bit."

***

I wasn't planning on asking my mom or dad for advice, originally, but after Suzi's comments about my being stuck in the '50s, I've changed my mind. I know my dad's mindset is more '70s-based and my mom, well, let's just say her take on things could prove interesting. Probably not very helpful, but interesting.

My mom's a big proponent of classical conditioning. Given her fondness for BF Skinner's experiments in behavioral psychology. You know, the ones where people give a test subject electric shocks of increasing intensity until their behavior changes. It wasn't about the shocks she claims, but about the concepts of reward and punishment. Food for reward and a shock for punishment. Until the bad behavior stop and is replaced by the desired behavior, which in this case meant dating me.

It wouldn't surprise me at all if she simply wants to hook Steve up (I prefer not to think of where she would attach the electrodes) and give him electric shocks until he asks me out.

I wonder if that's how she landed my dad? By using classical conditioning methods. The shocks would explain my dad's odd behavior, but how did she reward him?

I quickly decide I don't want to know. I'm not asking. Suzi will be over soon.

"Hey Dad," I say sticking my face into the garage. "Suzi's coming for dinner that okay?"

"Suzi!" he practically yells. "My favorite Vulcan."

Oh boy. But now was as good a time as ever. Dad was a man. He knows how men think. I think.

He'll know what to do.

"I honestly don't know what you should do," he says, when I explain my dilemma. "Every situation, every person, is different. But, I was watching a rerun of Friends the other day and Ross and Rachel ..."

I'm undecided on whether or not I like my real life relationships being compared to a TV sitcom. And, if you were going to do that, at least make the guy hotter than Ross. Make it Joey. Even Chandler. Just not Ross. The Rachel comparison, Jennifer Aniston, I'm fine with.

"So, finally, Ross says to Rachel: we were on a break. It's all about communication, Tessa."

There's a quick knock on the garage door and Suzi walks in. "Thought I'd find you guys out here. You know, in the man cave."

"Suzi!"

He's usually not THIS excited to see my friends.

"Live long and prosper," he says, holding up his hand and doing something weird with his fingers where he somehow separates his two middle fingers to form a V-shape.

"Peace and long life," Suzi replies, making the same odd hand gesture.

KMN. There's two of them, I'm outnumbered.

I try to make the hand gesture and can't. I'm better at single digit gestures, it would seem.

Chapter 28 — Steve

"Steve."

I look up from my laptop to see Suzi poking her head into my office.

"Mr. Osborne would like to see you in his office please."

"Sure. I just have to finish this email."

"Um. He said right now."

"Suuuure," I say, pushing my mouse aside and my chair back as I stand up. "What's up?"

I get a 'Suzi special' in return – a shoulder shrug. She doesn't know. Or doesn't want to tell me.

Only one way to find out …

"You wanted to see me, Mr. Osborne?"

"Steve. Close the door."

Not a good omen. He's seated behind his desk, this morning's paper in hand. He is clearly not a happy camper. Or any other kind of camper. His face is red and he reminds me of the personal emoji you can create that is literally blowing its top. He's hot about something and I've got a feeling I'm about to find out what.

"Did you know about this?!" he shouts, meaning to throw the paper down on the desk but accidentally (?) skidding it across the desk so that it hits my chest.

I look down at the front cover, read the headline and look up at my boss.

"Read it," he says. "Out loud."

At least it wasn't in City section, I thought, selfishly, or one of my writers.

Mayor stung by illegal snipe hunt scandal

by Anna Nordstrom

In an exclusive interview with this reporter, it was revealed today by an unnamed informant that Mayor Willard Westman took part in an illegal snipe hunt as part of a college fraternity initiation ritual more than 30 years ago. The news is especially shocking to many Minnesotans, a state that prides itself on respecting its natural resources. The source refused to reveal whether Westman actually killed any snipes, but the mere fact he was involved is disturbing enough.

It went on, but I don't really need to go any further.

"What's a snipe?"

"Exactly."

"Some type of bird?"

"They don't exist, Steve."

"Like a dodo?"

"No, there used to be such thing as a dodo. There's never been such a thing as a snipe. It's a made-up game frat boys like to play on new pledges. It's a wild goose chase. Except wild geese are real. Snipes are not.

"The entire story is bogus. We're a laughing stock, Steve. We'll be lucky if the Mayor doesn't sue us for millions. It's an election year. This. Is. Not. Good."

Precisely what I was just thinking.

"But … how?"

"I've already had a talk with Anna. And she actually told me the truth. It's not good. Not good at all.

"It seems your girlfriend …"

"We're not …"

He stops me with a raised palm.

"Yes, I know all about the two of you. I've been looking the other way for now because your work – and hers – hasn't been affected and her internship is just about up anyways.
"However, it seems Tessa plays hard both on and off the baseball diamond."
"What do you mean?"
I'm confused now.
"How is Tessa involved in this?"
"You don't know?"
"No."
"You didn't help her with this?"
"Help her with WHAT?"
What was going on here? Was I being accused of something?
"Tessa's the secret informant in the article."
I stare back blankly.
"She sent Anna misinformation somehow, probably from a public library PC or something. Anna says she picked up a scrap of paper off Tessa's desk with the source's online name and meeting details. Some kind of chat room thing is what Anna tells me. Never did like those things. It's all made-up. Every word. And Anna bought it. Her ambition got the better of her.
"The night editor will be lucky to keep their job. I spoke with Morty … and I'm letting Anna go today. Tessa's your employee and I'll let you decide what to do with her.
"My advice … let her finish out her internship and then we can have this conversation again. What Anna did was worse. I know she stole Tessa's story before – yes, I know – and she obviously didn't bother to fact check this," he slaps the paper on the desk again. "But …", he just shakes his head.
"I'll talk to her," I say as I get up. "Thanks."
"Sorry," Suzi mouths as I pass her desk.

Back in my own office, my brain is swirling with thoughts. Thanks? Thanks for what, I don't know. Thanks for making ME talk to Tessa? Thanks for not firing me even though I had nothing to do with it? Thanks for firing Anna? Thanks for not firing Tessa?

She probably deserves it. What she did is completely unethical in a profession where ethics and integrity are everything. On the other hand, she isn't REALLY an employee, technically, and her entire career is at stake. Plus, well, I like her. Or used to. I liked who I thought she was, before – but this, this changes things.

I get up and go to my office door, about to make a very difficult decision.

"Tessa, can you come in here a minute please?"

Chapter 29 — Tessa

I stop writing the obit I'm working on – Mr. Glenn Yearwood had led a long and interesting life – and head for Steve's office.

"Close the door, please."

I wonder what this is about.

"Any idea why I called you in here?"

"Um, because you like me?" I say, playfully.

He grimaces and sets the newspaper down in front of me. I haven't looked at it yet today.

I glance down, read the headline and look up again.

"Oh."

"Yes," says Steve. "Oh."

And then …

"What could you possibly have been thinking?"

To which I have no response. No intelligent one, anyways.

"I wasn't, I guess."

"You weren't. You guess," he repeats.

"Do you have any idea what this does to the paper's reputation? To our credibility as a news source? We could lose readers over this. Advertising dollars. We could get sued over this. This is serious stuff, Tessa. Very serious."

I have nothing to say. What can I say? Guilty as charged.

"I just came from Mr. Osborne's office. People are going to lose their jobs over this, Tessa."

I hoped one of them was Anna.

"I didn't mean for …"

"He thinks we should let you finish out your internship, wait until after your feature has run, and then decide."

Decide? Decide what?

"This way, at least you get your work experience complete and have a solid byline story for your portfolio."

Oh, so I AM going to need a portfolio. They were deciding what to do with me. And it didn't sound good.

It was about to get worse.

"Tessa …" he pauses. "Tessa, I'm not going to be able to be your friend anymore. This … this is unacceptable. You could have cost me my job, my career. I don't understand you, Tessa. This isn't like you. At least, I didn't think it was."

"I'm sorry."

What else could I say? I AM sorry.

If I could, I'd take it back. Not because I don't want revenge on Anna, but because of Steve. This was twice now, counting the $3,000 'N' incident, that I'd let him down.

I was counting on Anna's vanity – and lack of honesty – that she wouldn't admit she stole either my previous story or the fake information off my desk. In the end, she caved and admitted to everything.

She might as well, I guess. She's probably, hopefully, the one Steve talked about losing their job, so no reason for her not to sling some mud my way on her way out the door.

And I did kind of deserve it. I probably should have felt sorry for her, but I didn't. Don't let the door hit you on the way out, Anna. I never saw her again after that day.

But I have bigger fish to fry. AGAIN with the fish metaphors! Enough already, Tessa.

Steve doesn't want to see me anymore.

I know we're not really boyfriend and girlfriend – not like his mom thinks we are, and not like the whole office, other than Suzi, thinks we are. Never really were. We'd only had the one moment, the baseball tourney thing, if you counted that. And that dream kiss thing … which wasn't real anyhow. Just like the whole relationship, in the end.

"I'll tell my mom we're breaking up … and I'd like for you to tell anyone who you've either told or misled about the nature of our relationship the truth."

He's talking, but I'm not really listening. Something about no hard feelings, thanks for this and that, what's best for both our long term futures … blah, blah, blah.

So I could keep my job, for now, but not Steve.

How did I let it come to this? Why didn't I leave well enough alone? I had my story, why did I think I needed to teach Anna a lesson? Why did I not…just…grow…up? Why wasn't I more like Steve?

He'd never pull a stunt like this. Probably the worst thing he's done in his life is let his mom keep thinking we're actually dating. A couple. Which we weren't. Aren't.

Steve was so … real. And I, even my break-up was fake. Or was it?

Because for a fake relationship and fake break-up, the room sure reeked of the decay of a dead relationship.

There's definitely nothing fake about the way my heart it pounding, hurting.

"Tessa?"

"Sorry." My eyes are moist and I try not to look up.

I don't know what to say. And even if I did, I'm not sure I could say it right now.

"Me too," Steve says, his voice cracking with emotion. "Me too."

Chapter 30 — Steve

There's a chilly crispness in the air, a harbinger of fall. It's going to be getting colder soon. It already feels colder in the office.

Normally perky Tessa is morose. Listless. Cordial at best.

It's back to "Good morning, Mr. Sondergaard" instead of "Hey Steve".

And I'm back to … back to being myself. Alone. Without even my bowties to comfort me.

That's one thing Tessa was definitely right about. The bowties were very Mr. Rogers, while my new look, while still not 'cool' by conventional standards, is more Clark Kent-ish. The problem is, most women are looking for Superman.

I'm just me.

Or, like in the movie Tessa and I watched, a Hugh Grant and Julia Roberts rom-com called Notting Hill – I'm just a boy, looking for a girl …

But I wasn't, not really. Tessa had just, kind of, happened. What are the chances it will happen, like that, for me again? Probably will. Maybe. I'm still young. If I just be patient. Be a little more sociable. Like Tessa.

That's one thing about Tessa, she wasn't shy. Ever.

I wasn't shy at work, on my own turf, in my comfort zone, and certainly I was an expert interviewer, but to just start talking to someone waiting in a line or a crosswalk? Probably not going to happen.

But, then, she doesn't sweat the small stuff. She does what she wants. She goes for what she wants. Hard. And that's okay. Better than okay, it's a good thing.

She actually has a lot of really good qualities.

In fact, if I had to testify in court, I'd have to admit to being pretty impressed by how she planned and executed her revenge on Anna. Was it professional? No. Was it childish? Yes. Was it exactly what Anna deserved? Most definitely. I just wish she'd let me in on it … before it ran. We could have taught Anna a lesson without letting the story go to print. Had Mickey design a fake page to put on her desk. It was deleted from the website and digital edition immediately, but you can't delete print. That's the strength of the medium. And, in this case, also it's Achilles heel.

Or, to stick with the Superman metaphor, its kryptonite. My kryptonite.

Would I have gone along with it if she'd told me? I like to think so. Maybe. I don't know.

She obviously didn't think I would.

Maybe I would have. Maybe I would have talked her out of it. Maybe I'd have found a more, I don't know, mature, solution.

But she didn't give me the chance.

Maybe she was protecting me, in her own way, by not getting me involved. But why risk her own career, before it's really even begun, by pulling a stunt like that?

If that was the case, then she cared more about my career than her own, which … didn't make sense to me. Unless … no. We hadn't known each other that long. There was no way she… not the L-word.

Ah, well, it was probably for the best anyways.

It was simply a matter of time before she got a job In another town. Better to end it now, before we get too close. So nobody gets hurt.

This is more of a business decision anyways. Bosses can't date their employees. I should have nipped that in the bud long ago. Even Mr. Osborne had known.

And looked the other way, knowing, in his wisdom, that things would eventually run their course.

It was just a matter of time.

This was as far as I was going. This paper. Maybe, one day, Mr. Osborne's job, if newspapers survived that long. This was it for me. This town. Living with my mom.

After sacrificing my childhood. After all that hard work. This was it. The top of the mountain.

I once had a discussion with a classmate, one of the few in university who would talk to me, his name was Tom, about the definition of success.

"It's all relative," he said, "a matter of perspective. Perception IS reality. If you think you're successful, then you are. If your goal is to be a truck driver and you are, you're successful. If your goal is to be a journalist, and you are, you're successful. It's not the job that matters, it's about being happy. What makes YOU happy, Steve?"

I remember being a little taken aback by the question – I was still in my mid-teens. And Impressed by the worldliness of this 21-year-old with the long, swept-back hair and dark sideburns.

But here it was again. That question. Staring me in the face. Unblinking.

"What makes' you happy, Steve?"

Did I know, really? Did anyone? Probably. Did Tessa? Maybe. For me, writing makes me happy. It likely won't make me rich, but it makes me happy.

But not just any writing. I could never write a thriller or a mystery. I'm Steven Sondergaard, not Stephen King.

No, interviewing people, finding the truth and sharing it is what I like to do. I'm happy with my job.

I liked going shopping with Tessa. THAT made me happy, surprisingly.

I like playing baseball, but would anybody want me on their team if Tessa wasn't part of the bargain? Doubtful.

"Stevie?"

It's my mom's voice. I'm in the living room. I must have driven home from work, but I can't remember what route I took. Probably my usual one. Did I have the radio on? I can't remember any songs, just a lot of … thinking.

Way too much thinking. About everything. Work. Home. Mom. Tessa. Me.

"Is something wrong, Stevie, You don't look happy?"

"I'm not, Mom."

Chapter 31 — Tessa

Now I know what a zombie feels like.

Mindlessly sleepwalking your way through life every day, non-thinking, non-caring. In search of your next brain to eat. Or job. Or boyfriend. Or both. Maybe all three.

I wasn't planning on eating any brains – although with my dad's cooking methods you never know – but I sure feel, or, rather, don't feel, anything. Nothing. I feel … nothing.

It must be obvious I'm just mailing it in. I come in on time, I do my job, I go home. Nothing more, nothing less. I'm basically just putting in time, sticking it out, until my internship ends and my article is published at the end of this week.

Ste…Mr. Sondergaard must have noticed. He's certainly back to his stuffy old self. We barely speak.

It's probably for the best anyhow, long term. For me.

This paper. This town. Forever. That might be okay for a guy like Ste… Mr. Sondergaard, but I had plans. Big plans. They were always there. I'd just … thought … maybe …

No. That's crazy. He'd never leave this job. This town. His mom. Especially his mom.

I used to look forward to coming to work every day, but now I dread it. The ride in with Suzi is still great – I wish I had her positive outlook on life – and then it's all downhill from there.

Today, though, Suzi is … different. She seems upset. Like she's got something on her mind.

"What's on your mind, Suz?"

"What's on my mind?!" she exclaims loudly. "What's on my mind?! Hello?! Earth to Tessa, come in Tessa."

I keep driving.

"Don't you get it?"

"Get what?"

"You and Steve, dummy. You're blowing it. Why?"

"Um …"

"I'll put it the way your mom would, so you'll understand. When it comes to Steve, would you say you're:

A: Very in love

B: Somewhat in love

C: Maybe in love

D: Probably not in love

E: Definitely not in love"

"Um … all of the above?"

"That's not an option."

"He's mad at me."

"Mad, schmad, he's a guy. It will pass. Smile and he'll forget."

"He's not like that."

"ALL men are like that."

"Not Steve, he's … he's different. He's nice. He's a gentleman."

"He's a dork. And, if he loses you, he's not as smart as I thought."

"He's smart."

"If he's so nice, and smart, I ask again: why? Why are you letting this happen this way? So you got in trouble for what you did, so what? It's over. You were a bad girl. You went to your room for a timeout to think about what you did. Now get over it … before he gets over you."

"I don't think he wants to talk to me."

"I'll bet he does. Think positive thoughts and put them out to the universe. It's called manifestation."

"You don't know him like I do. He's not … normal."

"Not normal?! Not normal?! And just what the deuce IS normal? Or abnormal for that matter. You know, sociologically speaking, normal can be defined as those physical or behavioral characteristics or traits that are most common in a particular sample of specimens. For example, if you did a random survey of people and found that 75% owned a dog, then that makes owning a dog normal. For that population sample. By definition, anyone who doesn't own one is abnormal."

"Sounds reasonable, I like dogs. More than most people."

"But you get my point. Steve IS normal, in his world. I've met lots of guys, Tessa, take my word for it, Steve's about as 'normal' as they get. That's a good thing. I'd take normal any day."

"But he …"

"Even if Mr. Normal lives with his mom. He's kind to you Tessa. He respects you. I'll bet he … loves you," Suzi says, whispering the last two words, as if it's some kind of secret, or the car is bugged or something.

I'd take Mr. Normal too. But would he take me? I wasn't as sure as Suzi.

***

This week has gone by slower than a traffic jam when you have to pee. Painfully slow.

And speaking of pain, Mr. Osborne wants to see me. Again. Oh well, it IS my last day, one way or another. Maybe he just wants to wish me luck. Ya right.

"You want to see me, Mr. Osborne?"

"Have a seat, Tessa. I want to talk to you about something. A couple of things actually. The first, is this."

He slides the Friday morning print edition across the desk to me.

There, right on the front cover, across the bottom in a big, bold banner, is a promotion for my Home for Hope article. See story in today's City section. Extra coverage online. It wasn't supposed to run until Saturday.

I flip to the City section and there it is. I'd seen the layout proof, but it looks like there's been a couple of design revises since. No worries, it looks … awesome. Thanks Mickey. Thanks Steve.

Is it getting misty in here or am I … OMG … this is NOT happening. I am NOT going to cry in front of Mr. Osborne.

"I wanted to get it into our biggest circulation day. Reach as many readers as possible. This is great work, Tessa."

I'm in shock.

"Great?" From Mr. Osborne?

"Jenny just called …"

Uh oh, here it comes. The other shoe is about to drop. It's a great story, but ….

"And they've already received more than $100,000 in donations this morning, thanks to your article. I know it's not 'hard news' Tessa, it's not investigative journalism, but you can still make a difference. Even from the features department.

"The answers to all life's problems aren't on the internet, Tessa. It's not good enough to go to someone's Twitter feed for a quote. The same quote everyone else has. It's about the people, Toews. Always. You've got to talk to the people."

Okay, not what I was expecting. But … he's right. I really can make a difference in the world. One feature story at a time.

"There's an opening in features. Anna's old job. You start Monday … if you want it."

If I want it?! Boy do I want it!

"It's a step up from obits, at least the people you're writing about are alive." he laughs. "You'll have to let me know by the end of …"

"I'll take it!"

"… Today."

"It will include writing regular feature articles, advertorials and contributing to the monthly lifestyle magazine. Can you handle it?"

Can I handle it? Darn straight I can handle it.

"You'll report to Morty. Then you and Steve can see each other without it being a problem."

The look of pure shock on my face must be obvious. Of course it is, that's why he's grinning. It would seem the old goat – I mean the all-powerful Oz – sees and knows more than he lets on. Good thing he can't read my mind right now, or can he? Hmmm.

"Welcome aboard, and good luck," he says, shaking my hand while gruffly calling out another last name. "Schmidt! The new intern," he says, giving me a smile and a wink. "Don't tell them I'm a nice guy, Toes."

I laugh.

"Don't worry, I won't. And it's pronounced Taves."

Wow! This job, this town. The way this happened – manifested – Suzi!

This must be where I'm meant to be.

I can't wait to tell her.

And Steve. I'm going to tell Steve.

Chapter 32— Steve

"It's Tessa, isn't it?"

Wow. Bang on. What is it they say about a mother's intuition?

"You miss her, don't you?"

Right again, Mom.

"Oh, honey, I'm sorry. What's going on?"

I tell her the whole story. Everything. Finishing with my decision to break things off.

Come to think of it, it WAS my decision, wasn't it?

Tess had never really given any indication one way or another which way she wanted to go. I had done the breaking up, I tell my mom. This is my fault.

"Well, then, you'll just have to un-break-up, dear. Make it right. It's probably not too late, you'll never know unless you try."

Now even my mom was starting to sound like Tessa.

"If you want her back, you'll have to tell her."

Want her back? Do I want her back? Did I ever even really have her? We weren't really boyfriend and girlfriend, in the true sense. Of course, I've never had a girlfriend, so my only reference was the movies and TV. What little I'd seen. For a few brief moments I'd fancied myself as a bit of a Hugh Grant type, until I found out about some of his off-screen adventures. Maybe I was more the Cary Grant type.

And we certainly hadn't done the things boyfriends and girlfriends do on screen. Not even close.

Sure the odd hug, that kiss at baseball … which … was … now that I thought about it … incredible.

"I know you think it wasn't 'real', dear. That you were just pretending, for whatever silly reasons you young people have. But you weren't pretending to be happy. That was real. I've never seen you so happy. In fact, I'm tempted to call Tessa myself and …"

"Please don't, Mom."

"Or maybe her mother."

I can only imagine how THAT conversation would go. Prepare yourself for the full Freud/Oedipus lecture, Mom. That Freud was one creepy guy, if you ask me.

"Call her, Stevie. What have you got to lose?"

Nothing. Right now I have exactly nothing to lose. I've already lost it. Worse, I'd throw it away.

"Her internship's over, put the work stuff behind you. Now you can just be … you. Call her."

Maybe I will, if I can work up the nerve. If I can think of what to say. Maybe I should write it down first, so I don't get anxious and forget what I'm going to say. Expressing emotion is not my specialty.

"I will, Mom, thanks."

Maybe.

***

"Hey Steve-o! Got a minute? Good," Suzi says, not waiting for an answer and sitting down across from me.

"It's about Tessa."

Of course it is.

"About you and Tessa, actually."

"Suzi, I really don't think that's any of your …"

"Business? That's how you think of life, isn't it? Like a business. All formal and logical and black and white. A place for everything and everything in its place. Well, I've got news for you, Stevie-boy, life isn't black and white."

Stevie-boy?

"We live in a full color world, dude. Stop and smell the flowers. You're young, live a little. Go to a concert. Get a tattoo. Go to Vegas. Just. Grow. Up."

A tattoo? Me? But don't they hurt?

"In the meantime, while you try to figure out if you're a boy or a man, you're could lose something wonderful, something many people go a lifetime without ever finding."

I still haven't said anything. I haven't had a chance to. And my face must be betraying my confusion.

"I'm talking about love, dummy. L-O-V-E. Tessa is head over heels in love with you, in case you haven't noticed. No, of course you haven't. "

Tessa's in love with me? Did she actually say that? I wonder.

"Whatever," she shakes her head. "It's your life. But it's Tessa's too and I'm her friend. You can tell Mr. Osborne on me if you want, but that's how I feel."

Tessa loves me?

"Anyways, um, ya, that's it. Oh, Mr. Osborne wants to see you. Have a good day."

I still haven't spoken. Not a word.

Have a good day?! Thanks, hurricane Suzi. Not much chance of that, especially now … now that I know how badly I've messed things up.

Tessa loves me? Really? Me?

Is that what I feel for her, too? Love?

I have no idea what love feels like, but Suzi probably does and she could be right – this might be it.

I should talk to Tessa.

***

"You wanted to see me, Mr. Osborne."

I have no idea what about. Tessa's story ran – and looked great – reader feedback so far was incredibly positive. There's nothing else urgent going on.

"Steve, sit down."

Oh, so this wasn't going to be a short meeting.

"It's about Tessa."

Again.

"Sure. What about her? Her story looked great. Her internship is over. I assume we're giving her a glowing reference?"

"Better than that. I offered her Anna's old job in Features, and she accepted."

I stare blankly. Tessa was staying. Here At this paper. In this town.

"I know you too had a bit of a 'thing' happening ... it's all good," he waves off my attempt to interrupt and explain, "and that you broke it off because of this snipe hunt thing." Ah the great and powerful Oz. He DOES know all.

"I don't make a habit of getting involved in my employee's personal lives, Steve, you know that. But, I'm going to make an exception in your case. I know you've probably talked to your mom about this ... and I know Suzi spoke to you earlier. Yes, she came and told me. Everything. Sorry about that," he chuckles. "She's quite the spitfire. I like that about her."

I kind of do too, sort of.

"She certainly is."

"Anyways, Steve, this opens things up for you to see Tessa. For real this time. If you want to. As long as you're not her supervisor, there are no company rules about co-workers dating. I'm not telling you what to do ... I'm just ... yes I am, darn it! Talk to her, Steve. Don't let this one get away. And don't throw her back, either. She's a keeper."

Fishing metaphors are a big thing in Minnesota.

"I just about let Jenny get away. Would have been the biggest mistake of my life. She's the best thing to ever happen to me. I'm a far better person – a nicer, happier person – because of her. "

THIS was the nicer, happier Oz? Sort of like George Bush Sr.'s kinder, gentler machine gun hand – I'd hate to see the 'before' version.

But he's right.

And I don't need spider senses – Tessa's dad had mentioned them in regards to playing baseball and Tessa had explained the Spiderman reference to me – to tell me there's a trend happening here.

It seems Tessa and I are in love … and I'm the last to figure it out.

"Talk to her, Steve. A job's just a job. This is real life."

"I will. Talk to her. And Mr. Osborne … thanks."

I have to talk to Tessa.

Chapter 33 — Tessa

Not wanting to cause any unnecessary mid-day drama, I pop by Steve's office near the end of the day, but he's not in. Suzi says he left the office shortly after speaking to Mr. Osborne this morning and hasn't been back. I wonder what THAT'S all about.

Suzi looks a little guilty about something, but I don't have time to ask what.

I have to tell Steve … what, exactly?

That I'm hopelessly in love with him? Nope. Too much, too soon. That could send ANY man running back to his momma. No, I'd start with the job. I'm staying in town, I'll say. I'm not going to look for jobs at big city papers because I'm staying here. I'm working in Features now, so if you'd like to … to … to what? Be fake boyfriend and girlfriend again? Be friends? I'm not going to look for other jobs. I'm staying here.

But I'm not doing it for him, I'm doing it for me. Because it's right for me.

Sure you are, Tessa, the little devil on my shoulder says. Sure you are.

A million questions race through my mind, on a collision course with reality. Is he still mad at me? Is he mad Mr. Osborne gave me the job? Is he happy for me? Even a little bit? Does he feel the way I do?

Only one way to find out, I think, as I turn the key over in the ignition and head for Steve's house.

***

"Tessa!"

Steve's mom is home, but he's not. At least I don't see Brown Sugar parked out front.

"Come in, come in!"

His mom seems happy to see me, which is a good start. Better than good, according to Suzi, If the mom likes you, you're in.

"Suck up to the mom," she'd advised.

"Hi Mrs. Sondergaard. Is Steve around?"

"Tessa, please, call me Mary. We're well past formal titles, dear. No, I'm sorry, Stevie hasn't come home from work yet. He usually calls if he's working late, just to let me know whether to go ahead and cook supper or not, but I haven't heard from him. He's very fond of you, you know."

"Um ..."

"I've never seen him so happy as when he's with you, Tessa. I know, I know, you think I'm worried about you, someone like you, replacing me in Stevie's life. Yes, I watch Dr. Phil too. Not to mention have read the odd parenting book in my time. It's not easy being a single parent, especially when you're partially disabled. I know I've been a 'helicopter mom', trying to overcompensate, to be mother, father and friend. And in some ways, that hasn't helped Stevie. He's a little socially awkward, I know. But he's made huge strides lately. Because of you, Tessa. You make him happy. And that makes me happy too. All any parent wants is for their child to be happy."

Her eyes finally overflow with tears. And so do mine. No surprise there. Might as well start carrying a box of Kleenex around with me.

"I'm on your side, dear," she says. "You talk to Stevie when you get a chance, and in the meantime I'll put in a good word for you. I still have SOME influence around here, you know," she laughs.

"I will," I say, sharing a hug, "thanks."

I've only driven a few blocks when I'm startled out of my thoughts by my ring tone, which I recently changed to Ozzy Osborne's classic Crazy Train – my old high school baseball nickname.

Someone's calling in. Don't they know I'm having a moment?

"Hello," I say, trying hard to hide the emotion in my voice.

"Tessa, its Dad. Are you crying?"

So much for hiding my emotions.

"Are you okay? Where are you? Steve was here to see you. I stalled for as long as I could – I even showed him the old Abbot and Costello baseball comedy routine 'Who's on First' on YouTube. He didn't really seem to get it. Good guy though. Solid guy."

Steve was at my place. Steve was at my place!

That could only mean one thing.

He wants to talk. Yes, let's talk, Steve. Let's talk.

"Thanks Dad. I'm fine. Just had to make a pit stop on the way home. See you soon."

***

"Hi, Steve. It's Tessa."

"Tessa. Hello. I was just at your place. Talking to your dad. Well, he was doing most of the talking and I was doing most of the listening. I see where you get it from now. The talking. I mean, let's talk. I want to talk. Where are you?"

He sounds nervous. His mom is right, he sucks at this.

Luckily, I don't.

"I just left your house. I was talking to your mom. I'm on my way home."

"You're on your way home … then … we should …"

I hear a horn blast and that little car coming at me is flashing their bright.

"… Meet each other right … about … now!"

He hits the brakes and twists the steering wheel, leaving a short trail of rubber on the road as he drifts sideways across both our lanes – coming to a stop mere inches from my front fender as I grip my steering wheel tight and screech to a halt. The car behind him honks, pulls into the right hand lane and makes a rude gesture as they go by.

Talk about meeting somebody halfway!

There's not much traffic heading my way at this time of day, but Steve's stopped across the left lane on his side, causing a minor traffic jam behind him as cars attempt to shuffle over into the other lane to pass, many honking and gesturing as they do so.

"You're blocking traffic," I say, pointing at the growing line of vehicles.

"Tessa! This will just take a minute," he yells, opening his rear car door and reaching in for something. Something large. "I've got something for you."

He holds it up … and I'm crying again. Crap!

It's a mounted and framed glossy copy of my article in the paper. Just like Mr. Osborne used to do with his army feature stories. There's even a little gold plaque at the bottom of the frame with my name and today's date on it. And something else: "Love Steve".

So THAT'S where he was all day.

"Oh, Steve, it's beautiful. Thank you."

"I'm sorry, Tessa. About everything."

"I know."

"Mr. Osborne told me about the job. Congratulations."

"Thanks. And the answer is yes."

"Yes? But I didn't ask you anything."

"Yes, I'll be your be your girlfriend, silly, your REAL girlfriend this time. The answer is yes. Now pull off the road before you get run over."

Chapter 34 — Tessa

Our first official date as real boyfriend and girlfriend is today. Finally, we get to go on an actual 'date'.

It's been a whirlwind of a week at work, learning the new job. Thank goodness my new boss, good old Morty, from the ball team, has so much experience ... and unlimited patience. Unlike some people, who are threatened by young people and worried about protecting their jobs, Morty actually shares his tricks of the trade with me. Morty the mentor, I call him.

Steve's been busy too, working with the new intern. It's a guy this time, not that I was worried. Okay, maybe just a little.

I notice Steve's happier, though, and I definitely am.

We broke the good news to our parents, together, and my dad even suggested we invite Mary over for one of his world famous barbecues. I'll have to see what's on the menu that evening and give her fair warning. If he's in an Indiana Jones mood, we might be having monkey brains or goat eyeballs or live baby eels or something.

My mom tried to give Steve a quick Rorschach ink blot test, but gave up when Steve said they all looked like a bunch of bugs splattered on a car windshield. Score: Steve 1, Mom 0. I can tell she's intrigued by him. She'd probably like to hook his brain up to electrodes to see what makes him tick. But I generally save that for the second date. Kidding.

Steve's mom cried and cried and hugged us both. And then cried some more when I said I'd help Steve install a new stair-lift in their house. AS it turns out, she and Steve had talked about it, and he was building her an entire self-contained suite in the basement, with a stair lift

I no longer saw her as a barrier to our relationship, but as a compliment to it, a stabilizing factor. She may be frail physically, but Mary is as mentally strong as they come. She's had to be, and I respect her greatly for that. And for the son she raised into such a fine, caring young man.

We're going – surprise – to a Minnesota Twins baseball game at Target Field in Minneapolis. It's an hour and a half drive, each way, so we're making a day of it, taking in an afternoon game then going out for dinner and to a karaoke bar (my suggestion) where I'm going to sing Born to be Wild at the top of my lungs.

I don't wear a lot of makeup, but I put a little on tonight, just some eyeliner, as I wait for Steve to come pick me up.

"Hey Steve."

That's my dad's voice. Steve must be here. I didn't hear the doorbell over the lawnmower, which has now stopped.

"Who's on first?"

Daaaad!

Steve's voice now. "What's on second?"

"I don't know …" says my dad.

"… Is on third," they finish in perfect two-part harmony.

So he DID get it! Of course he did, he's got an eidetic memory – he remembers EVERYTHING. He was just toying with my dad all along. I imagined them working on an assortment of whacky electronic inventions out in the workshop. Maybe now slightly less whacky, with Steve involved.

"Okay," says my dad. "That's the secret password. Come on in and I'll call Tessa for you. Tessa! Steve's here!"

Yup, my parents have definitely never met anyone like Steve before. And neither have I. Because there's nobody quite like him … I'm the luckiest girl in the world.

"Now … you kids … have a … good … time."

My dad was trying out his impersonations again. I wasn't sure if he was going for a Star Trek-era William Shatner or that creepy Christopher Walken guy, but it was … haltingly accurate.

He can't help it, really he can't. He grew up watching the original Star Trek in the '60s.

"May the force be with you," says Steve.

Oh boy. Wrong sci-fi series, but at least he's trying.

"Did you bring your glove?" I ask, grabbing mine from the front closet.

"Just like you told me. I don't know why, though. I thought we were watching, not playing."

Ah Stevie-boy, you'll see. Stick with me, kid, you'll see.

***

I'd bought us tickets in center field, front row. Some people like to sit behind home plate, the better to see the one-on-one duels between pitcher and batter, but I prefer to sit out in field, where I can take in the entire game in one glance. I can see who's on first … oh no, now they have me doing it! We have hot dogs and sodas, it's a nice September day and there's lots of fans out. A perfect day for baseball, and our first date.

Towards the end of the third inning, one of the Twins hits a deep fly ball to center … really deep. I quickly whip my glove on and glance at Steve, he's hypnotized by the ball sailing high, higher than he's ever seen, and I'm sure, a tiny white dot against the clear blue sky.

He's not great at judging these things yet, but I can tell it's coming … right … at us.

It's over the wall, a home run, and the crowd cheers. I lean over the rail, reaching, reaching … and feel the ball hit my glove just as I feel my feet leave the ground. I'm going over the rail. It's a good eight feet down – this is going to hurt. But I caught the ball!

Suddenly, I'm … not falling anymore. It's Steve. He's got me. He's got me with those strong arms of his. I'm not falling. He won't let me.

"Nice catch," we both say at the same time, and then laugh. The crowd cheers again, as they replay my catch on the jumbotron. It WAS a pretty good catch.

"Don't worry, Tessa. I won't let you fall. Ever."

"Okay," I say, "but it's probably safe to put me down now." He was still holding me. This had to be the best first date ever. What could possibly make the day any better?

"Take me out to the ball game …"

It's the seventh inning stretch and apparently who's on first isn't the only thing my dad taught Steve. He knows all the words and belts them out boisterously. I'm hoping he picks a better song for karaoke tonight – maybe a Beatles tune – but at least he's singing. Out loud. In public.

The crowd is cheering again, and I look at the jumbotron to see why. There's Steve, center screen, larger than life, singing his little heart out. And there's me beside him. And there's the little heart frame around us.

It's the kiss cam. We're on the kiss cam.

I grab Steve's arm to get his attention and point to the big screen. He's startled to see us on there. It's obvious he's never seen the kiss cam before. Poor guy, doesn't know what to do … but I do.

"I love you, Steve," I say, as we have our first kiss – our first REAL kiss – in front of 30,000 people.
"I love you too, Tessa."

About the Author

Jade Anthony is the thirty-something-year-old, Houston-born daughter of an oil and gas geologist and her sociology professor husband.

She credits her mom for her love of shiny rocks, preferably diamonds, and preferably set in a ring; and her dad for her wealth of '70s and '80s pop culture knowledge – thanks to endless childhood hours spent watching old sitcom and cartoon reruns and listening to "classic tunes, dude".

Jade and her twin sister, Jane, also a writer, live in small home on a one-acre lot on the outskirts of Whitefish, Montana, big sky country, where they have a large garden, two dogs, two cats, two chickens and one rabbit (for reasons that should be obvious to any romance reader).

Never married, Jade is still awaiting her own Prince Charming – hopefully one with a twin.

Stop the Presses: My Boss is My Fake Boyfriend is Jade's first novel and the first of three novels and one bonus novella in the Stop the Presses young adult sweet romance series.

Published by Zanger Enterprises

ISBN # 9798364487117

Manufactured by Amazon.ca
Acheson, AB